UP AN OMEGAVERSE CREEK WITHOUT A PADDLE: A SWEET LESBIAN ROMANCE

CHAPTER 1: JESSICA

The backseat of my parents' car was cramped with three of us in it. I sighed, leaning my forehead against the car window, the better to stay clear of Summer's wildly gesticulating hands.

If I'd known my brother's best friend was coming along on this trip, I would have insisted on bringing my car too and splitting our group. These camping trips had always been a family thing, just my parents and my brother and I. No one had ever dragged anyone else along.

I probably wouldn't have minded so much if it was anyone but Summer. The three of us went to the same college, the best in the state, but that was all I had in common with them. My brother Aidan and I are like night and day in our personality and attitudes, so while he was practically attached to Summer at the hip, she and I had never really clicked.

I just finished up my junior year studying Neuroscience. Aidan still hadn't declared a major, and Summer was double-majoring in Environmental Studies and Omega Studies. Or maybe the second one was Political Science. Something to do with politics or government policy.

Don't get me wrong, I admire her passion for her causes, and her dedication to making the world a better place. I think it's very healthy to take such an interest in being involved in improving things. I just wish she wasn't so abrasive. She could be ferocious if she thought you had the wrong opinion, and would yell your ear off about omega rights or endangered species, or whatever had currently caught her interest.

In fact, she was doing that right now as we all traveled in the car to the campgrounds.

"So the salamander species in the caves near our campsite, only lives there. It's literally the only place those salamanders can be found, period. Yet, you think that the development company gives a shit about that? There are laws against it but like that's actually stopping them—"

On the other side of her, I could see my brother mouthing something to me. It looked like "Save me Jessica!"

I barely held back from rolling my eyes. He'd invited her.

I'm not heartless, I totally feel for the salamanders'

plight and all, but we were on vacation. Was it really the right time to think about the erosion of the cave ecosystems or whatever? It was bumming me out.

Thank God she'd said she was getting a cabin for herself and wouldn't be sharing ours. Initially I'd argued she should stay in ours (the waste of money rankled me, it didn't matter that her family was loaded and could afford it). But Mom and Dad had put their foot down on the matter.

They were convinced that there would be hanky-panky if two unrelated young people were under one roof together. It was ridiculous. Summer and Aidan had known each other for most of their lives and had never developed any sort of romantic interest in each other. Summer was certainly cute enough, with big doe-like brown eyes and a button nose. She'd chopped her ash blonde hair short recently but it looked good. It wouldn't matter how pretty she was though, my brother wasn't into omegas. Likewise I'd only heard about Summer going on dates with girls.

Neither one of them had cared about being housed separately on this trip. It's not like we'd be spending much time in the cabins anyway, aside from sleeping. Mom and Dad always dragged us out on hikes and kept us active, because 'You have time to loaf around and scroll on your phone the rest of the year, you can spend one week outdoors!'.

Not that Aidan and I minded, we loved these trips (one of the few things we have in common).

Now, trapped in a car with Summer and her biodiversity lecture, I was looking forward to arriving at the campgrounds more than ever. I did my best to tune her out and watched the countryside speed by through the windows. It was pretty out, peaceful, not a cloud in the bright blue sky.

Before long Mom was turning the car off the blacktop and onto the little dirt road that led to the outfitter's store. I moved my head away from the window quickly. With all the bouncing and jouncing we were undergoing from scraping along the rocky dirt road, being too close to the window glass was just asking to bang my head on it.

Fortunately the outfitter's wasn't very far along the road. We were pulling in before I could get too nauseous from the bumpy ride.

The store, a big log cabin near the riverfront, was packed. There were tons of tourists in their flipflops and bathing suits milling around outside as they waited for the buses that would take them to the dropoff point for the floating trips. In addition to handling the campsite and cabin rentals, this store also offered up canoe, kayak, raft and inner tube rentals for floating down the river. We'd be doing that eventually, but for now, Mom just wanted the keys to our cabins.

"You guys stay in the car, I'll be out in just a sec." she said.

"I want to come in!" Aidan said.

Mom gave him a forbidding look.

"What? I'll be bored out here and I want to buy stuff." he said.

"You can walk down and shop later, our cabins aren't far from here." Mom said, and got out of the car.

Aidan crossed his arms and huffed, but Mom was true to her word, and returned a few minutes later with a small keyring with our last name, "Hartwell" on the sticker attached to it. Summer's key was on there too, since she'd been booked as part of our group.

"See? That didn't take long." Mom said, and started the car back up.

A few more moments of being in the jolting, bumping car, and we were at the site of our cabins. Both of them were made of logs and rock siding, and the larger one had a covered porch with a little patio table and chairs. That would be ours. Summer's was the smaller cabin that was a few yards over.

We all piled out of the car and started grabbing our bags out of the trunk. Summer just had a single duffle bag, and she slung it over her shoulder and sauntered off to her cabin. The rest of us headed for the family cabin.

The front door opened into the living room, and I wrinkled my nose at the decor. It was very kitschy, every hard surface covered in little knickknacks, every end-table and even the dining table covered with doilies. Not to mention the plaid. The plaid was everywhere—the couch was plaid, the curtains were plaid (except for the kitchen curtains, which were plaid with roosters).

Some of the figures on the coffee table caught my eye. I sat my suitcase down next to the hideous plaid sofa and picked one up, turning it over in my hands. It was a little doll with a soft body and a porcelain face. This one was an omega, going by its historical costume. There was a beta and alpha in the set as well, and half a dozen smaller child dolls.

"Jessica, get in here and pick out your bed and dresser!" Aidan yelled, startling me.

I almost dropped the doll, but caught it just in time. I sat it back down on the coffee table to rejoin its family. Now it was time to rejoin mine.

Mom and Dad had already disappeared, probably to their room. I headed in the direction Aidan's voice had come from. Down the hallway there was only one door open among the four there. I poked my head through the doorway.

Inside the room were two beds across from each other, and two dressers right next to each other on the far wall. And Aidan, already inside and cramming his clothes into one of the dressers.

He looked over and noticed me.

"Just kidding, I already picked mine!" he said.

I snorted, and headed over to the dresser that he wasn't using. Unlike him, I took the time to remove my neatly folded clothes and put them into the drawers carefully, making sure they were in level stacks. One drawer for shirts, one for pants, one for underclothes and socks...I wasn't even halfway finished when Aidan was already done unpacking his things and racing back out the door.

When I was finished putting everything away, I went outside too.

CHAPTER 2: JESSICA

Once we'd all unpacked, we all piled back in the car and headed back to the storefront to sign up for one of the day's float trips. It was still mid-morning, so we had time to do a seven hour float. I was looking forward to it. Even though I'd gone with Aidan on one in the spring, it felt like that was ages ago.

After we'd paid for the canoe rentals, we walked down to the river to the launch site. Everyone was in their swimming clothes. Aidan and Dad were decked out in eye-wateringly bright tropical-patterned swim trunks. Mom and I both wore one-piece swimsuits. Mine was light blue to match my eyes.

Only Summer wore a bikini. I had to say it suited her form, which was very curvy for someone who was so short and slender, but that wasn't unusual for an omega. The dark purple of the swimsuit contrasted sharply with her pale skin. She always reminded me of someone that would be better suited for a fantasy novel than our modern world. Like she should be some Elven princess, or maybe a dark witch.

As we walked closer to the river, the rough dirt began to give way to rocks. Everyone in our family was wearing water shoes, because we'd been to this river many times on family trips in the past, and knew how rocky the riverbed and "beach" were. But Summer must not have known, because she was walking barefoot, not even in flip flops.

"Ow, what the hell?! This is nothing like the beach! Why isn't it sandy?!" griped Summer.

Aidan started cracking up. "You're such a princess, Summer."

She shoved him for that, making him stumble. "Shut up!"

"If you'd like, I can carry you until we get to the canoes." I offered.

Maybe it was the alpha in me, but seeing her discomfort itched at my brain. It bothered me.

Aidan laughed even harder as Summer's cheeks reddened.

"Or I can, if you don't think Jess is strong enough." Dad offered.

I was totally strong enough to carry a little slip of a thing like Summer. I'm tall even for an alpha female, and I'm on the university's basketball team.

Summer glared at us as she ground out, "That's not necessary. I can WALK on my own."

Yikes. We really stepped on a sore spot of hers. I'd forgotten how touchy she was about anything she perceived as babying her due to her omega status.

She had total helicopter parents who were extremely protective of her because of her secondary gender. She really had spent most of her life locked up like a princess in a tower. An angry complaining princess, but still one. When they were younger, Aidan and her had had to play and hang out at her house, because her parents wouldn't let her out of their supervision.

I could understand why she'd be sensitive towards anything she perceived as undue protectiveness or chivalry. I'd have to make an effort to avoid anything that might make her feel condescended to.

She continued to grumble under her breath as we walked, but nothing more was said. Finally, we reached the shore, which was littered with dozens of canoes and a couple kayaks. People were grabbing up canoes and launching left and right.

We all looked at each other, meeting each others' eyes and mentally considering how to pair off. Aidan was exempt from this calculation. He'd had his heart set on kayaking, and the rental company only offered single seat kayaks.

That left two canoes to split between my parents and me and Summer. Without saying a word, my parents headed towards one canoe leaving me and Summer automatically paired up.

I guess it made sense. While I would be happy sharing a canoe with either Mom or Dad, it might feel strange for Summer to share a canoe with one of her best friend's parents, someone twice her age that she didn't know very well. Not that she knew me any better, but at least we were around the same age and went to college together.

We shared a reluctant look, but after a moment Summer just shrugged. There was nothing to do but get on with it. We walked over to the same canoe, her steps picking their way across the rocks carefully since she still didn't have water shoes.

Inside the canoe were two ugly orange life jackets. I picked one up, sighing. I don't know who is supposed to look good in orange, but it's not me. It paired up poorly with my olive skin and wavy brown hair. Still, I know the importance of safety on the river. Even though this was a gentle one, and the water wasn't very deep in most places, all rivers could be dangerous and it was best to minimize risks.

I wasn't the type of person to break the canoe rental company's rules either. When a person or company says there was a condition on something's use, I just accepted it as law. Breaking the rules never occurred to me until I saw someone else doing so. They're the rules—you agreed to follow them!

Summer on the other hand did not seem to share my opinion on the necessity of life jackets. She gave the fluorescent jacket a glare, and didn't pick it up. I opened my mouth, then closed it hesitating. I didn't want to seem like a bossy overbearing alpha, trying to tell her what to do like she couldn't manage herself. But she really did need to wear it. How could I say it without seeming condescending?

While I was hesitating, a combination of Mom and Aidan came to the rescue.

"What do you think you're doing young man?" Mom's voice rang out, making everyone's head turn toward where she stood with her hands on her hips on the shore, staring down at Aidan.

He was already in the water, paddle in hand and about to take off.

"What?" Aidan said.

"You know you have to wear a life jacket." Mom said.

"But I'm in a kayak!" Aidan whined.

"And if you hit your head on an overhanging branch or run into a rockface, and fall unconscious into the water, is the kayak going to pull you back up?" Mom asked.

"Oh my God." Aidan ground out, but he began putting the life jacket on.

My eyes met Summer's rich brown ones. She held my gaze for a moment, then rolled her eyes and moved toward the remaining life jacket in our canoe.

That little bit of drama over, we picked the canoe up, each one of us taking an end, and begin heading for the water. Our ankles splashed into the river water. It was icy cold, but it felt good on what was already making out to be a hot day even for the summer. We set the canoe down into the shallow water.

"I'll take the back position, so I can steer." I said.

"Why should you get to steer?" Summer asked.

"Have you ever been in a canoe before? Or done any form of rowing?" I asked. My tone was neutral, genuinely curious.

I'd be more than happy to yield the dominant role in steering the canoe to her, if she knew her way around one. I suspected she didn't though, considering how overprotective her parents were. They weren't exactly the outdoorsy type either.

"No." she said, crossing her arms and scowling.

I just nodded. "Then it's probably best if you sit in the front for now. We can always switch later on if you want to, once you get a feel for it. It's usually best if the heavier person sits in the back anyway." I said.

I probably had forty pounds on her, due to being taller and having more muscle.

"Okay." she said, the scowl disappearing from her face to be replaced by a small smile. "That seems fair."

With that, she took her place in the front, while I held the canoe steady. Then I clambered in to the back, and we pushed off. I started telling her the basics of the techniques used, but she interrupted me.

"Aidan already told me some of this, when I said I was coming with you guys." Summer said.

"When did he invite you, anyway? He didn't tell any of us you were coming along." I said.

I was curious about that. Aidan's friends were well-liked by our parents, it's not like they would have refused to let her come along. Maybe it had been a last-minute invite? Or she wanted to avoid the risk that our parents would talk to hers.

I doubted Summer had told them she would be staying for a week in the woods with a different family. They wouldn't have gone along with it no matter what, but especially not when it was our family she'd be traveling with. They looked down on us and thought we were trash (which is ridiculous. We're a normal middle-class family. We just have a lot of junk on our lawn because Dad loves to tinker with things.)

Summer was almost nineteen, well into being an adult, but her family still acted like she was a naive child. Which was annoying for a teenager, but they probably would never change their view of her, even when she's gray-haired and wrinkled.

"Well," she hesitated, "Aidan didn't really invite me. So much as, I kind of invited myself along."

Her rowing stilled, and I let my own oar rest on the water as well. It's not like we had to row to keep moving. The current kept us drifting down the crystal clear stream. Rowing just moved us along faster. That was why Aidan was far up ahead, paddling furiously and about to go around a riverbend and out of sight. He was yelling enthusiastically about something, but we were too far away to hear what it was.

Mom and Dad were a little bit behind him, their rowing steady and easily synchronized due to years of experience floating together. I wasn't worried about Summer and I falling behind. We could always make up time by paddling fast like Aidan. I knew Mom and Dad wouldn't let us fall too far behind. They'd call out to Aidan and make him pull over with them at a good stopping point while we caught up.

So I sat in silence with her, waiting for her to put

her thoughts into words. It gave me more time to focus on our surroundings, admiring the way the breeze stirred the bright green leaves on the tree branches that overhung the river. I looked over the side of the canoe and peered into the clear water. The sun shone on it, revealing the river rocks, orange and brown and clean from the constant flow of the current.

My eyes didn't stray away for too long though, inevitably drawn back to the slender figure of the omega in front of me. She was still thinking.

"I guess...Well you know I'm majoring in Environmental Studies right?" Summer asked. Her voice was slow and cautious.

"Yeah, I think I remember you saying that." I said.

I kept myself from saying 'Everyone who gets within 40 feet of you knows that.' although I definitely thought it.

Summer was speaking again. "The thing is, as much as I care about encouraging biodiversity, protecting species' habitats, developing solutions to climate change, that sort of thing—I've never really been out in it." she said, her voice low like she was entrusting me with some dangerous secret.

I held back a smile.

"What do you mean?" I asked.

"My parents didn't let me go anywhere before

college. I never got to go on hikes, or travel to nature preserves, or go camping like your family is doing. I haven't seen what the world is like beyond the part that humans have built." Summer said.

"Oh." I said, catching on, "So that's why you wanted to come on this trip. To see what you've been fighting for."

"Yeah. I felt like a hypocrite, saying 'This is so important!' when I've experienced so little personally." Summer said, "That's why when Aidan mentioned this trip, I told him he had to bring me along. He didn't push back much, if anything he seemed happy. He said otherwise there would be no one to talk to except his boring parents and sister–oops. Uhh..."

"It's fine. I know Aidan and I's idea of what makes a riveting conversation is very different." I said. "Come on, let's start rowing again, we don't want to fall too far behind."

We picked up our oars and began rowing steadily again. She seemed to take to it pretty naturally (unlike Aidan, who had always flipped the canoe at least once every trip until he was sixteen). I didn't doubt that by the time the halfway mark had passed for the day, she'd be ready to take the lead in steering.

We caught up to the rest of our group before long, and our party floated along for about an hour before Mom called a break.

We'd arrived at a natural beach-like area, where the river bank was wide and sandy. We weren't the only ones to stop there, other people had ground their crafts in the same place.

We pushed our canoes back up onto the shore part way, enough so that they wouldn't float away.

Then into the water, this time on foot. Summer raced ahead of us, inspiring Aidan to chase after her to try and beat her. I looked at Mom, and could almost see her holding back a yell to be careful. The rest of us walked into the river much more sedately.

"Ahh, this is great. I was melting in that canoe." Summer said.

She was in the water up to her chin. Aidan was right next to her, floating around carefree.

"Maybe you can't handle the great outdoors Summer," he teased.

She swam over to him and seized his shoulders, trying to force him under the water. The two laughed and spluttered as they both struggled to shove each other under.

I studied her. Now that I was looking for it, her face and neck did seem flushed and reddened.

Their little play fight didn't last long, and to no one's surprise a now soaking-wet Aidan was the loser of it.

"Mom! Save me from this bully!" he begged as he swam away in our parents' direction.

They ignored him completely, continuing their conversation. Summer stuck her tongue out in his direction. Her brattiness was very cute to see. It was a shame I had to pull her attention away.

"Summer, did you put sunblock on? There's some in my bag if you didn't." I asked.

I wasn't trying to be condescending, but she herself had said she'd never spent much time outside. She might get mad at me again, but if it meant saving her from having lobster-red roasted skin for the rest of the trip, it was a risk I had to take.

"Yeah, of course. I'm not *that* much of a novice. I may not have been floating or camping before, but even I know you're supposed to wear sunblock outdoors." Summer said.

"Looks like you've managed to awaken Jessica's alpha instincts!" Aidan hollered over.

Summer slapped a hand across her face, groaning. She looked like she was turning even redder.

"Okay, looks like it's my turn to try and drown you..." I said to Aidan.

My face was menacing as I began walking toward him, the water sloshing in my wake. He screeched and ducked back behind our parents. His twiggy body was completely hidden behind our Dad's bulk.

I was very close now, but I didn't dare grab him right next to them. It's not that they really cared about our roughhousing, but Mom would get pissed if we splashed her. That was okay though. I was patient.

"You can't stay there forever little brother. And when you move away...I will get you." I said, my voice falsely saccharine.

A wave of water slapped against me, and I turned my head to see Summer approaching.

"I'll help," she said, "and if you hide there til we're back in our canoes, I'll help Jess catch up to you, and we'll flip your kayak over."

"Nooooooo! That's where my sandwiches are." Aidan cried.

"We have no mercy for sandwiches. So you should take your dunking now." I reasoned.

With truly heartbroken eyes, Aidan began moving away from our parents, accepting he was doomed. Summer and I grinned at each other, and followed him.

We had a good time, dunking him for quite a while, before we got bored of tormenting him. While he was swimming frantically away from us, Summer noticed something.

"What's that down there?" she pointed at

something.

I squinted in the direction she was pointing at. It looked like there was a large wooden sign posted a little ways downriver.

 "I don't know. Let's go check it out." I said.

We headed downstream, walking in the shallows. The sign was posted at a fork in the river. I had thought maybe they'd added a mile marker, but when we got closer I saw it was a warning sign telling us not to take one of the forks.

"I wonder what's down there that they would have closed it off for?" Summer mused.

"We've been on this river a few times before and it was never closed. It's probably just a strainer from the recent storms." I said.

"What's a strainer?" she asked.

"Something that's gotten into the river and is catching all the debris that floats by, but letting water pass through. Usually it's a big tree that's been blown down by a storm. They're dangerous, because you can get caught in the roots and pulled under, and get so tangled up you can't get back out." I said.

Summer shivered and stepped back from the sign, closer to me.

"Cold from being in the water so long?" I asked.

"No, if anything it's still too hot." she said, shaking

her head.

I wondered if that's all there was to it, or if she was spooked out by the warning sign and the possibility of getting caught in a strainer.

"Okay. Let's head back to the others, we'll let them know about the left fork being closed, and get some food. I'm freaking starving from all this rowing, it always works up an appetite." I said.

She nodded and followed me back.

CHAPTER 3: JESSICA

Lunch was a leisurely affair. Everyone, other than Aidan, shared freely of the food and snacks they had brought. Aidan had a massive pre-made sandwich that he jealously guarded. That was fine; I'd made brownies the day before and I wasn't going to give him one if he was going to be like that. (Not that I even wanted any of his sandwich, I could make my own.)

For sandwich fixings we had little rolls to make sliders with, and fluffy soft pita bread. There was a variety of different cheeses to put on them, from aged hard cheddars to soft spreadable goat cheese with herbs. We had fresh sliced salami, turkey, and ham, and even big slices of pepperoni to put on our sandwiches as well.

We also had fresh fruit on ice: chunks of pineapple and ripe strawberries and clusters of both purple and green grapes.

Amidst all this healthy fare, we also had the junk food. Bags of chips and pretzels, and dips to go with them. Cookies and pastries from the bakery downtown to supplement my brownies. There was no way we were going to be able to eat it all, not even with the extra fifth person we had along. But there was a fridge in the cabin, and we could always store it there and pack it up tomorrow for our hike.

Mom was adding meats to whichever bread we requested, while Dad sliced up the cheese. I was doling out servings of fruit onto the plates.

"Are you good with all this fruit, Summer?" I asked.

I wasn't sure what she liked. When she was hanging out with Aidan, I usually saw her eating snacks or pizza.

"Hmm? Oh yeah, it's all good. Give me plenty of everything." Summer said.

"Summer honey, I'm sorry we didn't bring anything special along to make you a sandwich with. If we'd known you were coming when we were doing the shopping, we would've gotten the stuff to make you a veggie sandwich." Mom said.

"It's okay, there's plenty here I can eat. And there's nothing wrong with a good cheese sandwich." Summer said.

I noticed now that one of the sandwiches Mom was lining up on top of the cooler already had the top bun on it as if it was finished, though it contained only cheese and lettuce.

"You're a vegetarian Summer?" I asked.

Somehow, that fact didn't surprise me.

She nodded. "Of course. Once I found out what goes on in factory farms–"

Aidan rushed over, enormous sandwich in one hand, and used his other hand to cover Summer's mouth.

"No. Oh no no no. We are not getting the 'meat is murder' speech while on vacation." Aidan said.

Whatever Summer said in response to that was too muffled by his hand for me to understand. It didn't sound complimentary though. I ignored them and took the finished sandwiches from Mom to put on the plates.

Once that was done I interrupted Aidan and Summer's argument to hand them both their plates. After that conversation ceased for a while as everyone was too busy stuffing their faces.

Once lunch was done and we'd packed the leftover food back into the coolers, Mom ushered us back towards the canoes.

"Come on everybody, we have to get going again. We need to get to the pickup point before sundown." she said.

This was met with a chorus of groans. We were all stuffed to the brim and just wanted to lay around. But she was right. Once the sun went down, the rental company would not be making any more trips to bring people back to the campgrounds. If we missed the last one, we would have to find our own way back to the cabins, and our canoes would have floated us ten miles down the river away from them.

So reluctantly, we all waddled back to our canoes. Or in Aidan's case, his kayak.

"It's no fair," he complained, "you all have help. I have to pull this thing along on my own. "

I snorted. "It all equals out. That kayak is way smaller and lighter than the canoes."

"I guess." he said, but still looked glum.

Maybe kayaking was a lonelier business than he'd anticipated.

"Now I can see I was lucky to be paired with Jess and not you." Summer said. "I bet you wish you could be dead weight and make someone else do all the work."

"That's not true! Besides, like you're one to talk. You're making Jessica do all the work. She's been steering." Aidan said.

Summer opened her mouth to respond, but I interrupted her before she got the chance.

"We were supposed to switch off, right? Did you still want to?" I asked.

"Yeah, I wouldn't mind giving it a shot." she said.

So we switched our positions in the canoe, with me climbing into the front and her sitting in the back. Then we used our paddles to shove the canoe off the shore and back into the water. The canoe began to drift forward, aided by our rowing.

"I didn't mention this before, because you said Aidan told you everything, but the person in front is also supposed to act as a scout. So I'll try and warn you if I see any obstacles up ahead." I said.

"Oh. I didn't really do that did I?" Summer said.

I shrugged. "It's not like we needed it. This is a pretty gentle river."

We paddled along for a couple more miles, the time passing pleasantly as the sun moved overhead in the sky. We weren't in a rush, and Mom, Dad, and Aidan had quickly overtook us again and disappeared from sight.

There wasn't much to say to each other, other than pointing out some of the prettier sights to each other, and giggling over the antics of some of the other river-goers we passed. This wasn't a "party river" but it still had plenty of people drinking and getting wild.

I did see something that, while maybe not extraordinary, was pretty awesome to get to see.

"Summer, look!" I whispered, pointing.

I didn't want to scare them away. A mother duck floated along not far from us, surrounded by the most adorable fluffy little baby ducks.

"Holy shit, that's amazing!" Summer said.

"I know, isn't it?" I said.

I cast a look back at her. Her brown eyes were wide and enraptured as she stared at the ducks. I smiled. It was somehow better, getting to see them with someone who had never gotten to experience such a wonder before. Seeing the wild animals in nature that we didn't get to see in the city, critters such as otters, big turtles, cranes, ducks, and the occasional fox running along, it never got old.

It was always a bit awe-inspiring, seeing them in their natural habitat, being reminded that we humans are not alone in this world. But it was extra special watching someone else get that realization. Being able to share it with somebody who also appreciated it.

We had stopped rowing for the moment, both of us wordlessly agreeing that we wanted to stay within sight of the ducks as long as possible.

But sadly, the current of the river carried us along. Eventually we rounded a bend and they were out of sight. But I knew there'd be more marvelous things to see ahead of us, there always was.

Another mile passed, and we caught up to Aidan. The much-famed kayak was upside down. Aidan was paddling around the water frantically, trying to snag bits of gear before they floated away.

"Here, let's stop and help him." I said to Summer.

We steered the canoe to the nearest river bank and parked it there. Then we headed back into the water on foot to help him grab the items that were floating away. He'd been hoarding snack-sized chip bags and now they were floating everywhere as he wildly grabbed after them.

Meanwhile I saved his sunglasses from sinking slowly into the river. Summer snagged the real treasure though, managing to grab the cell phone he'd encased in a plastic sandwich bag, before it could go under or float away.

"Really, Aidan? A Ziploc bag? Do you know how much that phone cost Mom and Dad?" I scolded.

"It's not my fault! Those little waterproof boxes are too expensive!" he said.

I covered my face with my hand. He really was too much.

"Besides, look at it. It's fine. The Ziploc bag worked." Aidan said, holding it up overhead triumphantly and waving it. Sure enough, not a single drop had made it through the bag's seal.

"But if it had hit the river bottom and snagged on a sharp rock, it could have ripped." I said, still convinced I was right.

"Well it didn't. And if you're so worried about it you can give me some waterproof boxes for my birthday. It's next month, hint hint." he said.

"Whatever, dork. Just don't flip your kayak again." I said.

He stuck his tongue out at me, but I ignored him. I'm way too mature for such juvenile antics. Summer and I headed back to our canoe. But instead of climbing in, Summer hesitated. She stood by the canoe looking at the rear seat.

"What's wrong?" I asked.

"I'm not sure I'm up to steering the rest of the way. I'm feeling kind of tired and dizzy." she admitted.

"Oh no!" I said, "Do you think you're just not used to all this exercise?" I asked.

She shrugged. "I'm not sure. My skin still feels really hot, even after going into the river again to get Aidan's stuff. Maybe I'm coming down with something."

"I didn't bring it with us on the float, but I have a first aid kit in my cabin. It should have a thermometer." I said. "When we get back, I can check your temperature."

"Okay. But for now, can you steer?" she asked.

I had no problem with that, so I took up my original position in the canoe. She sat ahead of me, her small figure looking ethereal in the natural setting.

We passed the next hour that way, rowing down the river and enjoying the sights. Eventually, we came to a wide part of the river where up ahead, there was a paved ramp leading up from the river to a road. Mom and Dad's canoe, and Aidan's kayak, were already banked on the shore. I could make out their forms sitting nearby. We'd hit the pickup point. I sighed.

Summer tilted her head towards me, nodding as if an agreement.

"I know. I don't want it to be over. " she said.

"If you liked it that much, you should come with us on our next float. It really is one of those things where it's the more the merrier. And we do this a couple times a year." I said.

"Maybe." she said. "I don't imagine this is a thing many people do by themselves."

She was right. There had been only a few people on the river traveling by themselves. And those had been mostly male alphas in kayaks.

"I've never came out here by myself." I admitted. "But if you don't want to wait for our parents to call another family vacation, you can always ask me or Aidan to come. We're always game." I said.

She smiled at me. "Really? Even if Aidan didn't want to come, you'd go with me?"

"Of course." I said. "I know you're Aidan's friend, but you and I got along alright this time, right?"

"Yeah. That surprised me. You always seemed kind

of...above it all, before." she said.

I knew what she meant. I've been called it all–nerd, know-it-all, teacher's pet, boring, stuck up–I'd never been very popular or fit in well with people my own age. I never seemed able to keep up with all the pop culture references and humor that everyone else did so easily. To be fair, some of that was probably my fault. I didn't find those things very interesting. I'd rather spend my time lost in a good book, conducting or discussing research, or being out in nature.

But despite what some people might think I didn't look down on others. It was something a lot of people had accused me of before, and I really don't get it. I do make an effort to try to be more approachable and to not sound condescending. Do I succeed? I dunno, but I must've done all right today, or Summer wouldn't be willing to go out on the river again with me someday.

To Summer I just said, "I'm definitely not above it all. Just outside it."

She laughed. She had a nice laugh, clear and high. Maybe she understood a little of what I went through. Summer is way cooler than me, but her interest in politics and activism is much deeper than most people's. If Aidan's reaction (and even mine, to some extent) is anything to go by, it probably turned people off the same way me eagerly asking my classmates if they'd read the latest issue of the *Journal of Neuroscience* did (what? They were fellow bio and pre-med majors– why were they even attending classes on the subject if they didn't want to keep up with the research going on? People are baffling. Hence my desire to study their brains and figure out what makes them tick.)

"I might take you up on that offer some time." she said.

I smiled. We continued rowing our way towards the ramp.

I was a little eager to take off back to the cabins. I was hungry again (What? it's all the exercise!) not to mention tired and sore-armed from all the rowing. But I was also filled with sadness and longing since it would probably be at least another month before I could be on the river again.

Summer and I pulled our canoe up onto the shore and got out. We hefted the canoe up and carried it away from the lapping water so it wouldn't get swept back into the river before the rental company could retrieve it. We left it lying amidst the dozens of other canoes that had been left by people who had finished their floats earlier.

"Come on, I can see the bus pulling up over there." I told Summer.

Looking amused, she followed me to where the rest of our group and a dozen other people were gathered around. A long, bright yellow bus was parking near them.

"A school bus?" Summer asked.

I shrugged. "How else are you going to get two dozen people back to the campgrounds?"

Everyone formed up into a line, and we boarded the bus. It was awkward, since a lot of the adults were much bigger than the child-sized bodies that the bus seats had been built for. I was lucky both Summer and I were slim, but Mom was looking downright squished sharing a seat with Dad, who despite being an omega is a really tall and broad guy. Aidan was the odd one out of our group, and ended up sitting with a stranger, a beta girl about our age.

The bus took off with a rumble, lurching down the rough dirt road to take us back to the store. By the time I'd been in the bus seat for five minutes I was already sticking to it in the heat, while simultaneously being tormented by the feel of river water dripping on my skin.

I had brought a towel, but unlike everyone else I wasn't sitting on it. I had my hair wrapped in it, because otherwise the water dripping from it would have been insane given how long my hair is.

Summer had mercy on me and rolled her towel further out across the seat toward me, so I could share hers. I stood up for a second, holding onto the seat in front of me with an iron grip to avoid falling, and then sat down. I had to scoot a little closer to her to be able to sit on her towel.

She wasn't much for conversation on the ride back. She spent most of it staring out the window at the trees and bushes flying by. It was all new to her so I understood. It wasn't a bad way to pass the time. Some might consider it a little boring, but I thought it was good to have some empty time where we could just sit and be, exist and enjoy our thoughts for a while. Too often there wasn't time to indulge in such tranquility.

The absence of distractions made me aware of more details. Like that Summer had a nice smell. It was a light flowery scent, but I had noticed it emanating from her while we were on the river. I wasn't sure if it was her natural omega scent or if she was wearing perfume. Surely it had to be natural right? The river water would've washed away any artificial scent sprayed on. Whatever its source, I found it appealing. Which was strange because I don't usually like the scents of omegas, preferring the more neutral smell of betas.

The bus finally reached the store, and everyone disembarked. Some people heading to their cars were probably driving home, but others, like us, would be heading on to campsites and rented cabins. We were all too tired and hungry to talk much on the ride back to the cabins.

Dusky twilight had given way to full night by the time we parked outside the cabins. They had automatic porch lights, and they switched on, providing some light as we walked up.

"Alright everyone, let's all get changed. Then meet back out here so we can discuss dinner." Dad said.

We went inside and got changed out of our swim clothes and back into regular shorts and T-shirts. I changed in the bathroom, while Aidan took the bedroom. I was the last one out, because of my futile attempts to tame my long hair, which had gotten tangled from us swimming.

By the time I went back into the yard, everyone else was clustered around the campfire. Or I should say, the spot for a campfire, because the actual fire was rather lacking. My parents had left Aidan of all people in charge of getting it started, which was a recipe for disaster if I'd ever heard of one.

"Jessica! Good to see you've finally joined us. Your father is going to barbecue for dinner tonight. Tomorrow, we'll go down to that general store down the road and pick up some more things." Mom said. "Summer, I know you're a vegetarian, but we have some potatoes and corn on the cob we can grill for you. And I'm going to make a salad."

Summer shook her head. "That's okay. I'm feeling pretty tired, and I think I'm just going to go to bed."

I looked over at her, studying her more closely. She

did look rather pale and kind of bleary-eyed. Oh crap! I was supposed to take her temperature. But I didn't want to keep her up if she was really beat...

"If you're sure, Summer." Mom was saying. "I'll make sure to save some back for you in case you change your mind."

"Thanks." she said.

I watched her trek back to her cabin. She seemed to move slower than she usually did. Were her muscles sore from all the rowing and swimming? Or was it aches from a fever? After the door closed behind her, I turned back to the group in front of me. Mom and Dad were busy getting the grill and meat ready, but Aidan's eyes met mine. He looked worried.

"She mentioned to me that she was feeling kind of feverish in the canoe." I said. "I hope she's not getting sick."

"I'll check on her later." Aidan said.

"Thanks." I said. "There's a thermometer in our cabin if you'd like to use it."

"We probably won't need it, but I'll bring it over to her." he said.

I nodded, and went to help Mom with making the salad.

Although my brother seems like a goofy and careless guy, when it comes to looking after the people he loves, he doesn't play around. I knew Aidan could be counted on to follow up with Summer. At the very least, he'd want to say goodnight to his best friend.

CHAPTER 4: SUMMER

Through the closed door of my cabin I could hear the others outside, Aidan and Jessica and their parents, sitting around the campfire and talking and laughing as they grilled up dinner.

For me, dinner wasn't an option. My stomach was trying to murder me. It churned and bubbled even though I hadn't eaten anything in hours. I couldn't have managed a bite of corn or potato salad or anything else Aidan's mom would have given me.

It was probably due to my high temperature. I didn't need Jessica to take it; I could feel the heat emanating from my skin.

I curled up on the couch in my cabin. The cabin's bedroom had a comfortable bed, but the thought of walking even a little bit further to get to it made me want to scream. I don't usually indulge in feeling sorry for myself, since it doesn't change anything. But I couldn't help throwing a little pity party now.

"Why me?" I groaned. "Why now?"

This was the first time I'd gotten away from the confines of my parents' house, or the overly-supervised omega dorm building at my university. And I had to go and get sick during it.

Sick if I was lucky–and I would count myself extremely lucky if this just turned out to be a very unfortunately timed bout of the flu, or maybe food poisoning from the lunch the others had shared out.

If it turned out this was all from getting overheated from the exertion of being active outdoors all day, I would consider myself more fortunate than a lottery winner.

But I had the sinking suspicion that what was wrong with me wasn't a stomach bug or the result of improperly washed fruit. What do you think of when you see that an omega is running a temperature? Heat. If you're like the rest of society anyway, that can't seem to keep its brains off of omegan reproductive functions.

I shouldn't be having a heat–I'd taken my daily dose of suppressants this morning, the same as I had done yesterday morning and the day before that. I haven't had a heat in years.

A lot of people claim it's unhealthy for an omega to not have a heat regularly, and I had had to fight my parents to be allowed on suppressants.

They were worried it would damage my

reproductive health, making me unable to make a good marriage (the only thing an omega was good for in their eyes). I'd held my temper then even though my tolerance for their bullshit was lower when I was younger.

I'd gathered the scientific evidence, articles and statements from well-reputed doctors who'd written on the subject, and made my case. I think my parents were less swayed by the psychologists and doctors' statements than by their notion that not having heats would make me less at risk to have sex before marriage. Having their daughter end up as an unwed pregnant omega probably featured in at least a couple of my mom's nightmares.

Although I hadn't mentioned it to my parents (why weaken my case?) there were real physical risks to not having a heat at least twice a year. Breakthrough heats for one thing. Even the most ignorant street dealer could tell you that you can't fight nature forever with suppressants.

I should've known my luck wouldn't hold. I'd been more fortunate than most omegas and never had a breakthrough heat before, not in all my years of using both prescribed and street suppressants. (I'd needed the bootleg suppressants because the doctors wouldn't prescribe an omega enough medicine to suppress heats all year long.)

Still, why now? Had I gotten a completely

counterfeit batch? I pressed my face into the pillow, trying to ignore the way my body was trembling all over. It was days like this that made me wonder if my parents and society were right. If I should just give in and accept my "place". Stop trying to fight a battle that it seemed I would inevitably lose.

But even wracked with pain from what was likely a heat, I knew I would never give in to what they wanted for me. I just couldn't do it. I wouldn't last longer than a day as a "good" omega. Obedient, smiling, eyes always downcast. Meekly married off to whatever alpha my parents decided was best for me—which probably meant whichever alpha had the most money and standing.

This was hell, truly hell. The heat made my body so sensitive that it hurt to be touched. Every brush of fabric against my skin was like sandpaper rubbing against it. Every smell, no matter how pleasant it was and how much I'd appreciated it before, was now overpowering to the point of being revolting.

Even the air seemed to agitate my skin. And there was nothing I could do but wait it out.

I gritted my teeth to hold back from crying aloud. An eternity seemed to pass like that, lying there sweating and panting, chewing my lip to shreds to keep from making any noise that might draw the others out of their cabin and over to mine.

I couldn't let the others know, it would ruin the

whole trip. Someone would have to take me back to my parents' house, and I couldn't stand the thought of that. Poor sick little omega can't even handle a single day in the outdoors.

I didn't want to change how Aidan's family thought of me. I liked them, and I didn't want them to start perceiving me as fragile and pathetic, someone to be pitied and babied.

It especially bothered me to think that Jessica's opinion of me might change. I usually don't give a shit about what any alpha thinks, but Jess had turned out to be pretty cool, for someone who was a total dork and managed to also be a jock of all things on top of that.

I felt guilty about it now, but I'd always hated her a little before today. We didn't run into each other often, since she was in a different year and we were in different majors, but I'd see her at Aidan's dorm room sometimes. Usually when he needed help with a paper or some project he'd left til last minute. (I can't judge my buddy for that; I'm almost as bad a procrastinator.)

Jessica was always able to help him, even if it was a class she hadn't taken and a subject she had little interest in. She was smart, which is a trait I usually admire, but somehow it'd come across as obnoxious to me. She'd seemed like kind of a know-it-all.

She'd help, but she always had an air of "I don't

know why you can't see what the issue is, isn't the answer obvious?". A sort of earnest cluelessness that drove me nuts. She'd always lecture Aidan on not starting his projects earlier too.

Top that off with her being on the college's basketball team and being an alpha (the lucky winners in the genetic lottery), and she really seemed to have it all, without having to make any sacrifices or struggle. She was even good-looking, if you like tall slim muscular alpha girls (which unfortunately, my stupid omega body and brain did).

Spending a whole day with Jessica had changed my opinion a lot though. Maybe it was being outside of a competitive environment like school. Or that I'd interacted with her enough to realize what I'd taken for aloofness and condescension, was really just awkwardness.

She might seem like she has it all but she's not very smooth when it comes to other people. Kind of ironic, for someone who wanted to be an expert on the human brain.

Today I had seen that she was kind and considerate, and could be a lot of fun. She was someone I would like to spend more time with and get to know better.

I thought I had done well on the river and earned her respect as far as being capable of handling myself in the outdoors.

But now she would see me as an omega that couldn't cut it for even a day away from civilization, having to be taken back to the city as my omega biology overwhelmed me. Not to mention what my parents would say when they found out...

I'd rather run off and live in Antarctica than see their faces when I told them I'd came back early due to being in heat. They had been outraged I had left on this trip at all. (Which is why I told them I was leaving over text message when I was already at Aidan's house. Ha!) The amount of "I told you so"s I was going to get wasn't funny though.

I lay there on the couch picturing my parents' disappointed faces and their scolding tones, for what felt like an eternity (when the pain wasn't making it impossible to imagine anything). But it was probably only a few hours before the sounds of everyone talking and eating outside died down. Shortly after it fell silent out there, I heard a very soft rap at my door.

"Come in." I croaked.

It had to be Aidan. No one else would check on me so quietly. If it was one of his parents, they would've called out and knocked loudly and openly. Same with Jessica. Only Aidan would have been able to tell that something serious was wrong with me.

Sure enough, when the cabin door creaked open,

the figure that stepped out of the darkness into my temporary home, was the short beta guy that was my best friend.

"Aidan." I said.

He carefully closed the door behind him, making sure it didn't make any noise.

"Summer, what's wrong?" he asked, stepping closer.

"What do you think is wrong?" I asked.

I managed to sit up, and he sat down on the couch next to me. He peered over at me, studying me. I'm sure I looked as sweaty and disgusting as I felt.

"You don't look so good." he said. "You coming down with something? Or did you finally get a breakthrough heat?"

"I'm pretty sure it's that last one." I said, rubbing my forehead. "Nothing else comes with this kind of oversensitivity."

Popular media (and old as dirt cultural beliefs that stuck around like a bad smell) would have you believe heats were all sexy fun times for omegas. And maybe they are for some omegas.

But for a lot of us, there was no upside to them. Instead we just suffered from extreme oversensitivity and migraines, and on top of that, the increased strength of our scents could bring annoying alphas around to bother us.

Aidan sighed. "Well, we knew it would happen someday."

"But why today? What a bunch of bullshit." I said.

I know I probably sounded whiny, but I felt entitled to be so. Just the sound of my own voice and Aidan's, both pitched so low as to be nearly a whisper, slammed into my head like a gunshot.

"It could be worse. At least classes are over. Can you imagine if this had happened during finals?" Aidan asked.

I could. That would probably be the second worst time for this to happen. I'd never been a grade-grubber, but I still didn't want to do badly. Although this semester I'd done well enough in my classes that even bombing finals wouldn't have made me flunk out.

"There is no good time for this shit. I can't believe this is happening." I complained.

"Well, it is." Aidan said.

"No shit." I said.

Thanks Aidan. Very comforting.

"What are you going to do about it? Do you want to ask your folks to come get you, or would you rather have Mom or Dad drive you back?" Aidan asked.

"Oh hell no. I am not going back." I said.

I scowled just at the thought. I was probably

making that angry bitch expression that my mother was always telling me to wipe off my face, because "no one likes an ill-tempered omega".

"What, do you like it so much out here in the woods that you're just going to live here? There are a lot of trees you could chain yourself to." Aidan said, smiling.

If moving even an inch wouldn't make me feel so much shittier, I would have grabbed one of the throw pillows and hit him with it. Usually I love the nonstop banter I can have with Aidan, but right now the situation was so not funny that any sort of joking about it enraged me.

"You know what I mean. I'm not letting this ruin the vacation." I said.

"It's not a big deal," Aidan said, "it'll take like, half a day off of Mom's vacation to drive you home and then come back here."

"I know they would do it," I said, "but aside from putting them out, how is it fair to me?"

He spread his hands out in front of him in a "What can you do?" gesture.

"I know what you mean Summer, but you're not going to be able to enjoy anything like this. You look like you're going to fall over and drop dead." he said.

I rolled my eyes. Then I groaned. Youch! Who knew rolling your eyes could hurt?

"I'm not saying you're wrong," I said, "but maybe if I can tough it out a little longer, it'll end before the week is up. Then I can enjoy a little more of my time here." I said.

"Is there any way I can convince you to let Mom or Dad take you home? Any chance you will budge at all on this, even a little?" Aidan asked.

He was well-acquainted with my stubbornness. He had told me before I was the most stubborn person he'd ever met, and he's not the only person I've heard that from (my mother says it on a weekly basis). I took it as a compliment. It meant I wasn't easily pushed around in a world that was always trying to make me follow the path everyone else wanted for me.

"Not the slightest." I said, crossing my arms. "I won't change my mind, and that's final. Are you going to tell your parents on me?"

Aidan's parents were so much cooler than mine, but I still couldn't see them letting me ride out my heat here. If he told them, the chances were good that they would insist on taking me back, or even worse, might call my parents.

I couldn't just out-stubborn his parents either. While Aidan didn't have any authority to make me leave, they did. The company that rented out the cabins had insisted I have an alpha sign off as my chaperone. I was only able to rent my cabin because Aidan's mom had signed that she would be responsible for me. If she decided to revoke that, I wouldn't be able to stay here any longer.

Before I could stress myself out any more, Aidan gave me his answer.

"No, but it's going to be hard to hide this." he said. "You might be able to stay inside and avoid everyone for a day or two, but any longer than that and Mom will insist on talking to you."

That was the crux of the problem. I would have to avoid *everyone*. Aidan was the only beta in his family. All the others had the heightened senses of an alpha or omega. Even if I hid my pain and acted normally, they could discover I was in heat by my scent alone.

I might be able to fool Jessica, but Aidan's parents had more experience with omega heats since Aidan's dad is an omega. They would probably find me out in seconds.

"Well, heats can be short. Sometimes just a day or two." I said.

I don't know who I thought I was fooling, me or him. What I said was true, but it was more complicated than that. There are a ton of variables that affect the length of omegas' heats. The omega's age, their personal biology, the frequency of their heats, whether they had a permanent mate, and whether they were regular users of suppressants...There were also myths, like the much-romanticized idea that discovering your so-called fated-mate and nesting with them would end your heat early, which was obviously just the usual sexist propaganda of "meeting the right alpha will solve all your problems!" in an appealing fairy-tale package.

I figured that was about as likely as me sprouting wings and flying, so I focused on the facts.

Most of the variables were working against me. I'd gone a long time without having a heat, and heats tended to be longer and stronger if you'd gone a long time without one. I was also single, and had never had even a temporary mate, let alone a long-term bond with someone.

"Maybe the suppressants I've been taking will help with that. They're still in my system, maybe they'll counteract it some?" I mused.

My reasoning was shaky and I hated how unsure I sounded.

Aidan looked away, his eyes sliding past me to focus on the wall behind my head. He always did that when he was thinking, as if he didn't want to lock eyes with someone while he was deep in his own thoughts.

I let him think. Aidan could come up with some pretty ingenious solutions sometimes. He had plenty of experience getting himself into and out of jams. Meanwhile, I was kept busy torturing myself with mental images of being dragged off in disgrace by Aidan's mom.

After a few minutes, Aidan turned back to me.

"I think we should tell Jess." he said.

"What? Why?" My voice came out loud even to my own ears, and I winced in pain.

Lowering my voice I continued, "She'll run straight to your parents!"

My opinion of Jessica may have changed for the better, but it didn't change the facts. She didn't have a rebellious bone in her body and was the opposite of a rule-breaker. Cover up something that could blow up in all of our faces, to satisfy the silly whims of an omega? No. She would do what seemed logical and correct to her: ratting me out.

"She wouldn't." Aidan said.

I raised my eyebrows and just looked at him.

"Don't give me that look, I'm serious. She may seem like a dorky Girl Scout, but she's covered for me before and not snitched on me to Mom and Dad." he said.

"That's great Aidan, but this is a little bigger than you sneaking out to go to Josh's party or to a concert with me on a school night. She's your sister, not mine. Just because she's covered for you doesn't mean she would go out on a limb for me." I said.

"You are really negative, you know that? I haven't even told you yet why we should bring her in on this." Aidan said.

"Okay, I'll humor you. How could telling Jessica about this possibly make it better?" I asked.

I sat back to wait for his explanation, and bit back a whimper as a jolt of pain shot through me. I'd leaned too fast and hard against the couch. It made me seethe; why should I have to hobble around like an eighty-year-old lady?

"There are many benefits to telling Jessica," he began, "Mom and Dad trust her way more than they do me. For some reason they think she is more mature and responsible—"

I snorted.

"So she can help us run interference and keep them off your back. She is also, in case you haven't noticed, an alpha." he said, emphasizing that last word as if it were meaningful in some way.

"You know the idea that omegas become sex fiends during heats is bullshit, right? I don't actually need an alpha to sleep with." I said.

I narrowed my eyes at him. I expected better of him than to believe such lame stereotypes.

"I know that!" Aidan said, "But the presence of an alpha does help shorten heats. Dad always says Mom being around him during his heats ends them faster. There's science behind it, hormones and pheromones and all that." he said, flapping a hand dismissively.

I was still skeptical, although he could be right. A lot of folk wisdoms had truth behind them, even if the people didn't understand the real reasons they worked.

I wouldn't know about this one personally. My parents were an alpha–beta pair, so I hadn't grown up around another omega. I couldn't say if my alpha mom's presence would've helped speed up my heats. My parents always locked me in a "heatproof" room during my heats.

No one was allowed contact with me, not even to drop off a meal. Instead the room was always stocked with meal replacement shakes, granola bars, and bottled water. It was a miserable, lonely hell, and one reason I'd been so eager to get on suppressants and stop having heats.

"I still think she'll tell." I said.

"And I say she won't. Just give her a chance, okay? Her help could be the difference between you getting away with this or not." Aidan said.

He seemed convinced, and it wasn't like I had a good alternative plan.

"Fine. But if she tattles on me, you're going to owe me so big. You'll have to write all my essays for next semester." I said.

"Uhhh..." Aidan was chewing on his bottom lip.

"What? You said you were sure she wouldn't go to your parents." I said.

"I am sure!" he insisted.

Under his breath he muttered, "I hope."

"Just go get her. The sooner we get this over with, the better." I said.

I wanted to know if the axe was going to fall on me or not. If I was going to be betrayed and sent away in disgrace, better to get it over with.

"Alright," he said, rising up from his seat and heading over to the cabin door. "I'll be back with her."

I could only lay there on the couch like a limp noodle, hoping he was right.

***

I was jolted out of my light doze by the sound of harsh whispers drifting in from the open window next to the door. I couldn't make out what they were saying, but they were speaking quickly, their tones tense and argumentative, talking over each other until the other shushed them.

I was just glad I didn't hear the voice of their mother or father. So Jessica hadn't ran straight to her parents' bedroom to hurry them out to save the wayward, heat-stricken omega.

Maybe Aidan was right and she was more trustworthy than I gave her credit for. But I wasn't ready to put all my faith in her yet. She might only be here to verify Aidan's story, then she would be off to ruin my vacation.

The cabin door swung open, and they walked in. I could hear what they were saying now.

"Aidan, this is crazy —" Jessica was saying.

"Don't tell me Jess, I've been saying the same thing. It's Summer you'll have to convince." Aidan said.

Jessica's gaze swiveled toward me. Somehow, despite having been pulled out of bed, her long chestnut-brown hair looked perfectly smooth. How did she do that? Some kind of product? She looked neat and put-together, even in comfy pajamas. She had on an oversized baby blue T-shirt and black sleep shorts that ended midthigh.

She looked way too good to be seeing me right now, considering I was at my worst. I knew the heat had probably made my skin all blotchy and my hair was probably sticking up all over like a hedgehog's quills from my sudden nap. It really wasn't fair. Not that I'm the kind of vain omega that cares about my looks or anything.

Though maybe Jessica has a soft spot for pitiful looking omegas. Her expression softened when she saw me.

"Summer, how are you?" she asked, keeping her voice pitched low.

"I feel like ten pounds of shit in a nine-pound bag."

I said.

Jessica huffed, laughing a little. "You must not be feeling too bad, with that answer."

I scowled at her. Just because I wasn't reduced to a weeping damsel in distress didn't mean this heat wasn't painful, annoying, and humiliating.

"Can I sit down?" Jessica asked.

"Make yourself at home." I said. "I'm not going to jump on you."

"That's not what I meant–never mind." she said.

She sat down on the couch next to me.

I knew I was being unfair and taking my crankiness out on her, but I felt like I was going to crawl out of my skin. It wasn't just the heat, it was the uncertainty. The not knowing if having her here was a huge mistake, or if there was even the remotest chance of her agreeing to help. And if there was a chance, what would I have to say and do to get her to agree to help? I wanted this to be over already, so my nerves could calm down and I could go back to sleep.

Aidan settled down on the floor near the coffee table.

"So, you're planning on staying in your cabin until your heat is over, and you don't want anyone to know you're in heat, other than Aidan and I?" she asked.

Her voice was perfectly level, her expression as smooth and calm as a lake. It irritated me to see her keeping herself so carefully controlled, like 'Oooh, better walk on eggshells around the hysterical omega!'.

"More or less." I said.

I crossed my arms. It wasn't just because Jessica made me feel defensive. Doing so let me bury my fingers in the flesh of my upper arms and grasp them in a tight grip, keeping myself grounded from the pain that wanted to pull my focus away from this important conversation.

"Feasibility of keeping this a secret from my parents aside...Why?" she asked.

"Why what?" I asked.

Did she think I wanted to have my first vacation away from home ruined? That I wanted to be sent home like a child who couldn't handle summer camp because they got too homesick?

She spoke up, answering me, "Why wouldn't you want to go home? Studies show most omegas prefer to spend their heats in a familiar environment. It gives a psychological sense of security during a biologically vulnerable time-"

"That's none of your business." I cut her off. "But I'd rather pass my heat in this cabin, or my dorm room, or a public fucking bathroom than the house I grew up in."

She had nothing to say to that. The silence hung heavy in the air, laden with tension. Aidan seemed immune to it, or at least he was hiding from it by staring at his phone. It was still wrapped in the plastic sandwich bag.

Jessica opened her mouth as if to speak, then closed it. Then opened it again.

Her lips were rosy pink. How dare she have such a perfect mouth? And use it to spew out typical alpha ignorance at me. 'Most omegas are like this, why aren't you Summer?' Like I'd never heard *that* before.

She was talking again. I braced myself.

"Okay. Maybe you have your own personal reasons for wanting to stay here, and that's totally valid–"

That was so condescending, but at least she wasn't arguing with me about it or demanding I tell her why I didn't want to go home so badly. I would've lost it if she did.

"But you still aren't going to be able to keep this a secret for long." she continued.

"Aidan said your parents would stay off my back for a couple days." I said.

"He may be right about that, but that's not a solution, that's just delaying the inevitable. Unless —are your heats usually very short?" she asked.

I bristled. My pessimistic nature and self-awareness of my own back luck made me want to say no. But the truth was I didn't really know. The few heats I'd had in the past had been short. But I hadn't had a heat in years and my body could have changed since then.

Not that I was explaining all that to Jessica. It was none of her business. Also, she would flip out if she knew about the illegal suppressant use. That would kill any hopes of her helping with this or at least keeping it quiet.

"They're uhh, kind of irregular so it's hard to say. " I offered up as an explanation.

She pursed her lips, her mouth a thin line of seeming disapproval. Or maybe I was being oversensitive and she was just thinking hard.

"Gambling on the slim possibility that you might have a short heat is too risky. You're just as likely to have a longer one, then everyone will find out anyway." she said.

"That's where you come in." I said.

I leaned forward towards her. "You are my ace in the hole. Something that will help tip the odds in my favor."

"What, you think I can get my mom and dad off your back for an extra day or two? I don't see much point in that, the week will be more than half over then..." she trailed off.

I grinned. "No. I have a better use for you. You,

my dear *alpha* friend, are going to make my heat shorter."

"Me?" Her dark eyebrows rose high on her forehead. "But what can I...Oh! You've read the studies."

Her face lit up as she came to this revelation. She looked so ecstatic, I almost hated to burst her bubble.

"I assure you, I have not." I said dryly. "It was something Aidan mentioned to me, that having an alpha's presence around can shorten heats." I said.

Jessica nodded. "It's an old wives' tale, although in them it usually includes sex–" she stopped, blushing hard.

"Go on." As miserable as I was, I couldn't help crooking my lips up at the sight of her flustered face.

"Well. Um. Anyway, they've started doing studies on it recently to see if there's truth to it. And while it will need more research to understand how it works, it does seem that being in close contact with an alpha during a heat tends to make it shorter. It also lessens the intensity of negative symptoms. There are some really fascinating ramifications for this in evolutionary biology, it's clearly the opposite of what the researchers thought the findings would be—"

"Get to the point, Jess." Aidan cut in.

So he was listening, even though he hadn't looked up from his phone once. Jessica glared at him. Then she turned back to me.

"They found that the mere presence of an alpha in the same room as an omega during their heat would have this effect. But it was amplified when there was skin-to-skin contact. I don't mean sexual contact, although it can be that. Any kind of touch; completely platonic skin-to-skin contact like hand-holding was just as powerful." she said.

Despite Aidan's warning to her, she continued to info-dump about the research. I might be interested in listening to her some other time— Jess did have some neat facts sometimes—but my patience for it now was nil.

I was on pins and needles waiting to see if she'd join us in our scheme. I needed the confirmation that the axe wasn't about to come down on my neck, at least not yet.

I cut in when she paused for air. "So, you can see exactly why we need you then." I said, before she could continue talking about the studies.

"I mean, I can see what you're getting at. But I think you may be expecting too much. I'm not your family member or even a close friend Summer. In most of the studies, the effect was stronger when the alphas and omegas knew each other well and were very compatible. Also the research on this topic is still in its early days, there's a lot we don't know yet." Jessica said.

"I don't see the problem. Think of it as advancing scientific knowledge. A case study, a little applied research." I said.

"Are you really trying to use my geeky side to win me over?" she asked.

There was a light in her eyes and a little smile on her face as she spoke.

"You catch on quick. I should have known you were too smart to take the bait. " I said, smiling back at her.

"Eww. Would you two stop nerd-flirting and make up your minds? I want to go back to bed. Also, you don't have a 'geeky side' Jessica, you're a geek through and through." Aidan said.

We turned identical burning glares his way. I was too weak to do it myself, but Jessica was totally reading my mind when she picked up a stray ball of paper from the coffee table and lobbed it at his head.

"Ow! What the hell?"

We both ignored him.

"I still think this is a bad idea." Jessica said, "The sane, responsible thing to do would be to tell our parents and to take you back to your parents' house for the remainder of your heat."

My blood began to boil at her prim attitude.

I opened my mouth to tell her exactly what I thought of that idea.

She put a hand up in a 'stop' gesture, and continued before I could get a word out. "But! You are an adult and should be able to make your decisions for yourself. Even if I think they're terrible decisions."

"So you'll help me?" I asked.

Hope coursed through me, easing some of my dread.

She sighed. "I know I will probably regret this and it will blow up in our faces like a typical Aidan scheme, but yes, I'll help you."

I didn't correct her assumption that Aidan was the mastermind behind this. I could always take credit if it went well. And if it didn't...Typical Aidan, right?

I was so happy I threw my arms around her. Then I fell back, groaning. "Owwwww."

Jessica's hand shot out, steadying me. I gave her a grateful look as she helped me settle back against the cushion, her touch mercifully gentle.

"Wow, your body must be really sensitized from the heat. Dad usually doesn't have any problems moving around." Jessica said.

Her dad hadn't abused suppressants for years, and he had also lived with an alpha mate for decades. But I didn't say that aloud. I'd only just convinced her to help me, I wasn't going to scare her off now.

"Don't worry about it," I said, waving off her concern, "it's always like this at first. It will get better."

I hoped.

CHAPTER 5: SUMMER

Jessica laughed. It was soft, not a real giggle, and I could just barely hear it. It wasn't loud enough to hurt my hypersensitive ears, or keep me from falling asleep. So there was no reason it should bother me.

But it did. I scowled at her. She didn't even notice, which was probably for the best. It was rude of me, especially since she was only here in the first place to help me. I was just too miserable to play nice and hide how annoyed I felt.

Maybe it was because when she laughed, even completely silently, her chest would do a little shake and I could feel it.

We were on our backs with our sides pressed together, lying together in my bed. She had one arm wrapped around my shoulders, and the other was holding up a thick hardback book.

I didn't see what could be so funny in it. The book

looked like it was on a boring nonfiction subject, primate behavior or something. Jessica was so weird.

I stared at her as she read. There was nothing else for me to do. The only TV in the cabin was in the living room, and I couldn't watch it right now anyway. The motion on the screen would make my head hurt.

I watched her for some time, as she turned pages and her eyes scanned the lines. She was deeply immersed. Finally she looked over, just a quick glance as if to check on me. She looked startled when she noticed my intense gaze that was dead set on her.

"Summer! Sorry, I thought you'd be asleep." she said, letting out a nervous chuckle.

I was glad to see I wasn't the only one feeling awkward about the situation. I'd started to like Jessica more after our trip down the river together. But when aching and in pain, I didn't like anyone at all.

No matter how much I might come to like Jess, it didn't change the fact that right now we were little more than acquaintances. Acquaintances who were dressed in very short pajama shorts and tank tops, the better to facilitate skin-to-skin contact, and we were cuddled up in bed like a couple who'd been together for years.

Despite how different her and I are, neither one of us was the type to fall in bed with a near stranger. It was a shame because it would have made this situation easier to bear, because at least one of us would have felt comfortable.

"It's kind of hard to fall asleep in this situation." I said.

"Would you like me to turn the lamp off?" she asked.

"No." I said, my voice flat.

The lamp wasn't a problem. It had a warm yellow glow that was comforting if anything. Having a light on never kept me from falling asleep.

Even Jessica could tell I was pissed off from the tone of my voice. She blinked at me.

"What's wrong?" she asked.

Then, before I could answer her, she hit her forehead with the heel of her hand.

"Duh! Sorry, I am so slow sometimes. I should've brought you a book too! You must be bored." she said.

I gritted my teeth. I was bored, but that wasn't the point. Wait, what was the point? What did I want from Jessica? Her to comfort me? Was I craving an alpha girl's attention? Couldn't be me.

Whatever it was I wanted from Jess, I wanted her to just *know*. Because I didn't know, or at least I couldn't articulate it well. But that wasn't fair to her. It wasn't really fair to anyone, but especially so in Jessica's case.

She was one of the most oblivious people I've ever met and over the years I'd watched her miss pretty much every subtle hint or clue anyone gave her, and a lot of ones that weren't so subtle. Not being straightforward with her was a recipe for frustration. Her father was the same way— sarcasm and irony went right over his head. They didn't mean anything by it, I knew they didn't do it on purpose.

And this time, she was doing me a massive favor. The least I could do was try to communicate clearly.

I let out a slow exhale. I was going to try this.

"I don't want a book. I think reading would give me a headache—well, it would make the one I have worse. I think I'd like it if you—if you'd keep me company. Like, active company, not just being in the same room." I said.

There, was that so hard? Of course, now my nerves started playing up. What would she say? Maybe my request was entitled. Maybe I was a spoiled brat of an omega demanding everyone's attention, just like my parents always said.

I held my breath while I waited for her response. With every second that she sat there with her brow furrowed, saying nothing as she thought over my words, my dread ratcheted up. I became more and more certain that she would say something along the lines of 'Isn't it enough that I'm here? Now I'm supposed to entertain you?'

Never mind that Jessica had never once been mean to me. Well, she'd rolled her eyes once when I'd been haranguing everyone in her family to go out and vote in the municipal elections. (What? Local elections matter too!)

Finally her mouth opened, and she spoke slowly as if every word had been carefully considered and chosen.

"I see what you mean. I'm sorry, that was rude of me. Mom always tells me a book out at the dinner table is as impolite as Aidan being on his phone when we eat. This isn't a meal time but I can see how the same sentiment applies? Kind of like I'm closing myself off from communication by hiding in the book. It can make people feel ignored. Or so Mom says."

Guilt rose up like a tidal wave and crashed over me.

"Jess, you have nothing to be sorry for. I should be apologizing to you. I'm just acting crabby over nothing because I'm in so much pain." I said.

"No, it's not nothing." Jessica said. "Besides, I shouldn't be reading right now. I just do it when I'm nervous, it's like a reflex at this point. It lets me forget what I'm anxious about. But I'd like to get to know you better, and if I have my nose buried in a book, I can't do that."

"You want to get to know *me* better?" I blurted.

I found that hard to believe. Not because I thought Jessica was snobbish or looked down on me—everything I'd seen from her on this trip, from agreeing to help me out to being patient with my crankiness, all pointed in the opposite direction of that.

But why would a smart, athletic, pretty alpha girl like Jessica think I was worth getting to know? I was sure she didn't look down on omegas in general, but me, this particular omega? Most girls like her wanted nothing to do with me, not even as friends.

Who would want to be around a rebellious omega who didn't care a bit about seeming well-mannered or submissive? Who instead of batting their lashes coyly at alphas, stared directly at their eyes in challenge? I wasn't flirty or flattering, I was bossy, demanding, and (although I'll never admit it to anyone) needy.

I know I come across as nothing but trouble. No one has ever been interested in me for anything other than my family's money, except for weirdos who think they'd enjoy the "challenge" of breaking a headstrong omega's will.

But Jessica must have seen something in me that was different from what so many others saw. Or she was just an oddball like Aidan, that enjoyed hanging out with misfits.

"Well yeah. Why wouldn't I? You're awesome Summer." she said, without a hint of irony, the sweetest smile on her face.

I could feel my face heating up, and the urge to duck my head down and hide my gaze was overpowering. Only long habit kept me from doing so, but I couldn't stop the warm pleased feeling from spreading through me.

"Tell me more about how awesome I am." I half-joked.

Jessica followed my request literally. "Well, you have an amazing sense of fashion—"

I snorted. There was no way I was letting her continue under that delusion.

"Pfft. I look like a hippie and a time-traveler from the Victorian era got together and had a baby. And that baby grew up and decided to honor both its parents' fashion tastes. While drunk and blind."

It was kind of true, but in a good way (at least in my opinion. And Jessica's too? Wow.) If I thought my combinations looked bad, I wouldn't have put them together and worn them. I couldn't deny my look was...eclectic, though.

After all, I did have my own credit card to get as

creative as I wanted with (my parents still paid the bill every month). I mixed up my regular mall finds with custom-made replicas of Victorian era clothes, and hired shopping services to get me cute things from overseas that normally wouldn't ship outside of their country. But if I saw nice handmade clothes and hemp accessories at the local Farmer's Market, I grabbed those too.

I expected her to laugh at my exaggeration, or else say something like 'You know your clothes are awesome, quit fishing for compliments!' like Aidan would. But typical of Jessica, she did neither.

"I wouldn't know." Jessica said, shrugging. "I have no fashion sense at all."

"Shut up!" I said. "You look fine."

It was true. Jessica had never been a fashion disaster like her father, who could come up with some truly bizarre outfits. And not bizarre-on-purpose to make a statement like I sometimes did. You could not convince me that Jessica's father wasn't colorblind.

Meanwhile, Jessica usually dressed very normally, in sporty, preppy clothes. The sort of fashion I might turn my nose up at, but there was nothing embarrassing about dressing that way. It was just a little lacking in excitement. In high school she'd blended in perfectly with the other girl athletes, and it was probably the same now that we were in college.

Now Jessica was the one blushing, tilting her face downward and picking at the bedspread, unable to meet my eyes. It was a very cute look on an alpha. Why couldn't more of them act like this?

I had no idea why she was reacting so strongly to what I'd said though. Surely Jessica of all people wasn't one of those girls who was convinced she looked horrible all the time despite being very attractive? I'd never gotten the impression she cared about looks or fashion at all. Too much of a nerd.

"Can I tell you a secret? You have to promise me you won't laugh." Jessica said.

"Sure. Confess away." I said.

I was intrigued. What dark secret could Jessica be hiding?

She took a deep breath. When the words came out, they were so rushed I could barely understand what she said.

"My mom picks out all my clothes."

She buried her face in her hands. I almost laughed, but I'd promised her I wouldn't so I bit my lip to stifle myself. It wasn't what she said that was funny, but rather the way she was acting like it was a war crime.

I reached out and tugged her hands away from her face. She let me.

"Why?" I asked.

"Because I have no fashion sense! Just like I said!" Jessica said. "There were so many times that Mom and Aidan stopped me from leaving the house, because they said I was committing crimes against fashion."

"Aidan can be an ass." I said.

She nodded, but continued. "I think they meant well. Once I started middle school, kids started to give me crap over it. So I asked Mom to help me pick out some basic things that I could mix-and-match without any risks. A capsule wardrobe, more or less."

"That is so sad." I said.

"I know. I'm pathetic." she said, covering her face with her hands again.

I pulled them away again.

"Not sad because of your fashion sense or your taste. But sad that they kept you from dressing how you wanted all this time." I said.

"Yeah, it is." Jessica said. "But what could I do? How you present yourself is important in life. I wasn't creating the impression I wanted to give. It's not like I wanted people to think I was cool or hot or something. Just...not have my appearance detract from my actual qualities and the things I care about."

I could see her point. Studious, earnest Jessica would have wanted to be taken seriously. Not laughed out of the room for wearing plaid pants with a polka dot shirt. Yeah, I'd seen her dad wear that before. Apparently Jess had inherited his (lack of) fashion sense along with his social awkwardness.

"Well, if you want some tips, I can take you under my wing." I promised.

Maybe it was a bad idea to make a commitment like that. I couldn't be sure that Jessica really wanted to know me better. She could just be acting nice to me and humoring me because I was in heat. And even if she did have a genuine interest in me, a couple days with my grumpy heat-stricken self might send her running.

Jessica perked up. "Would you really do that for me? I'd love your help. I wasn't lying about liking how you dress. You make a very strong statement, you know. I wish I could be that confident about the kinds of clothes I like."

"Definitely, it's a date." I said.

Shit, why did I say it like that? A flush spread over my already heated cheeks, and a matching rosy tint rose on Jessica's face. Open mouth, insert foot Summer.

"Uh, a date like an appointment, I mean. Not like a romantic, dinner-and-candles date. That would be weird." I resisted the urge to bury my face in my hands. Must. Salvage this.

"We'll go to the mall and pick out some clothes you actually like. But I'll help you steer clear of any disaster combinations." I said.

I must have not made a complete fool of myself, because Jessica smiled.

"Thanks Summer." she said.

"It's nothing. Now, you were telling me about all the ways I'm awesome...Surely it's not just the clothes I wear that's impressed you." I said, pretending to preen.

The slight movement made the pain flare in my joints, but I ignored it. I was having a good time talking to Jess, and I was not about to let my body hold me back.

"No, that's not what I admire the most about you. I hope this doesn't come across wrong, but you're really strong-willed for an omega, one of the most opinionated ones I've ever met. I like that though, that you have your convictions and won't back down on them." Jessica said.

Someone thinking it's a good thing that I'm bossy and opinionated? I was tempted to pinch myself. Maybe I'd fallen asleep and was having one of the weirdest dreams ever.

Then again, Aidan and I had always gotten along like a house on fire and he usually found my stubbornness funny, not annoying. Jessica was from the same family. Maybe they were all unusually chill?

I would have to reflect on their weird family quirks later. The silence was stretching on beyond what was comfortable and Jessica was twisting the hem of her tank top, waiting for me to react.

"No, it's fine. I'm going to take that as a compliment." I assured her. "I have plenty of things I like about you too. I'm not going to say you're awesome—alphas get told that way too much, sorry—but you're pretty cool for an alpha." I said.

"Gee, thanks." she said, laughing.

"I'm tired! And my brain is fried from this heat. You have to take that as a compliment too, because that's how I meant it." I complained.

"That is true," Jessica said, "whatever an omega says during their heats, goes."

"That's a severe overcorrection." I said. "Just going in the opposite direction of the usual bullshit about omegas in heat."

"It's what Mom always says, about Dad's heats." Jessica said.

Okay, I could totally see Jessica's mom saying that. Her mother totally spoiled and pampered her omega husband.

"That would be a dangerous policy to follow with

me." I said.

My mood was improved now, after talking to Jess. Our conversation had relaxed me and it felt like some of the stress had drained away. But I knew I could be a cranky omega at the best of times. Being in heat only worsened that.

"I'll keep that in mind." Jessica said.

I yawned. "Of course, the only thing I'm in danger of right now is falling asleep."

"Oh, are you getting tired? We can try and sleep some." Jessica said.

"Definitely." I said.

She picked up her book from where it was laying on the bed cover, and laid it on the nightstand.

"Lights off okay?" she asked.

"Sure." I said.

On, off, I felt like a freakin' disco ball could descend from the ceiling and flash strobe lights everywhere and I'd still be slipping off into dreamland within seconds. Exhaustion had hit me with the subtlety and speed of a freight train.

Jessica switched the lamp off, and darkness fell over the room. I should have felt uneasy, curled up against a strange alpha in a dark room during my most vulnerable time. But I didn't. I felt safe, and warm, and perfectly at ease.

I'd been a little worried that I wouldn't be able to fall asleep under the unusual circumstances. But it only took me a few moments to drift off in Jessica's arms.

CHAPTER 6:
SUMMER

When I woke up, it felt like I'd been boiled in hot water and then left out in the sun in a desert somewhere to dry. My eyes felt sandy and painfully dry, and my mouth wasn't much better. My body was an oven throwing off disgusting amounts of heat. I'd kicked the blankets off of myself at some point in the middle of the night.

It took me a moment to remember where I was — a rental cabin, on a trip with Aidan and his family. And the reason I felt like I was melting like candle wax, was because I was in heat.

Fuck. The bright sunlight pouring through the window over the bed told me I'd slept in long enough and it was time to get up and face the music. I'd fallen asleep curled up in Jessica's arms. Where was she?

The sound of a feminine voice humming drifted down the hall to my ears. The smell of coffee, delicious delicious coffee, hit my nose and told me what she was up to. The thought of eating might make me want to hurl, but the day I turn down coffee is the day I'm dead.

I eased my way off of the bed slowly, careful to avoid any sudden jolts or anything that might trigger a sharp ache. The pain seemed to have subsided a little, which made no sense, considering I was further into my heat. But whatever. Life gives me few enough breaks, I'll appreciate the ones I get.

I gingerly picked my way down the hallway, my fingers trailing along the wall, ready to lean on it if I experienced a bout of dizziness or pain intense enough to make me lose my balance.

When I finally made it to the little kitchenette off of the living room, I was greeted with the pleasant sight of Jessica, still in her sleep clothes, frying something in a skillet on the stove.

Whatever it was smelled sweet and doughy. Normally I might find it tempting, but right now it was anything but. At least she'd had the good sense to not fry bacon or eggs. There was no way I could stand the smell of all that meat and grease right now.

I couldn't begrudge her breakfast though. Just because my stomach was upset didn't mean she should go hungry. Besides, I would get compensation for my suffering in the form of coffee. As a consolatory treat, Jessica couldn't have done better.

I pulled one of the tacky camping-themed mugs out of the cabinet, and headed over to the coffee pot. Jessica noticed me then.

She spared a quick look over her shoulder at me, and cheerfully said, "Good morning!"

"Figures. I should have known you'd be a morning person." I grumbled.

"Well, it's only morning in the informal, relative sense. In that you just woke up, so it's your morning. Technically, it's already noon." Jessica said.

She flipped the food in the skillet with a spatula. It looked like a pancake.

I raised my eyebrows. Noon? How had I slept for over twelve hours? Normally I can't sleep for shit. I struggle with a double whammy of insomnia and being an incredibly light sleeper when I do manage to get to sleep. Maybe my heat had exhausted me so much it beat my sleep problems into submission.

"Don't drop any more bombshells on me before I've finished my coffee." I said.

"Okay," she said, "let me know when you're ready for your pancake."

"Not having one. There's no way I can eat right now." I said.

"I know it's hard, but if you managed to eat something it might settle your stomach some." she said.

"Oh, you know how it is huh?" I said, rolling my eyes.

She huffed. "You know what I mean. I read about it in a guide book on caring for omegas during their heats."

"Why did you read a book about caring for omegas?" I asked.

That was a stupid question. Jessica probably read the encyclopedia for fun. A book on omega care wasn't that far out there for someone who seemed curious about everything. She seemed like the type who liked to be well-prepared and plan everything out ahead of time. Jess would probably be an omega expert long before she even met the one she'd marry.

That is, if you could become an expert on omegas by reading books or doing a bunch of research. Which you can't (despite what many arrogant alpha doctors and scientists believed). It was amusing to think of a newly-wed Jessica getting a wake-up call in how little she really knew about omegas.

"Because I'm helping an omega through their heat?" she said, raising a brow.

Once again, Jessica had surprised me and made me feel a little ashamed of my assumptions.

"When did you have time for that?!" I asked.

"Well, not all of us sleep in until noon. I woke up around seven this morning and there wasn't much else to do. I didn't want to turn on the television and wake you up." she said.

"Thank you." I said.

That had been thoughtful of her. People were rarely considerate of me. I was so used to having to get angry and push back to not have my needs completely ignored, that gratitude was an uncommon experience for me. You didn't feel grateful towards people you had to browbeat into treating you decently.

"So, did you just happen to have an omega health book laying around?" I asked.

Lucky coincidence if so.

"No, of course not. Mom and Dad made a rule ages ago that I can only bring six books along on any of our trips. None of the ones I picked this time were about omegas at all. So I bought an ebook and read it on my phone." she said.

She'd bought a book just to be able to help me through my heat better? I didn't know what to say to that. No one besides Aidan had ever given a shit.

Then she began putting the pancakes onto plates. The presumption of it made my hackles rise. Still, she couldn't make me eat it. If she thought she could force this poor little ailing omega into anything, she was going to find out otherwise.

When she picked the plates up and headed over to the dining table, I followed her. There were only two dining chairs for it, and I sat down in one. She set the plate with just one pancake on it in front of me. I scowled down at it. At least she wasn't so ignorant as to expect me to have a regular appetite.

Jessica had a whole stack of pancakes on her own plate. Maybe she was that ignorant and had just wanted to hog most of the pancakes for herself. That was a completely unfair and uncharitable thought, but I was starting to get pissed again.

There was a small pitcher of maple syrup on the table, and she began pouring some of the syrup on her pancakes.

"Go on, try them. I swear I'm not as bad a cook as Aidan." she said.

"I'm not eating them," I said, "I'm not hungry at all, I never am during a heat."

"Alright." she said.

"Alright?" I asked.

I eyed her suspiciously. An alpha just taking my word like that, and not trying to push me into doing whatever they thought was best? Was I in some kind of mirrorverse? Jessica might be cool but I would never stop expecting her to reveal her true colors. It's just how alphas were; every one of them I'd ever met had let me down.

Jessica shrugged. "You don't have to eat the

pancake if you don't want to. But then, you won't get the prize."

"What prize?" I asked.

What crazy crap had this alpha been up to now?

"If you eat even just a bite of your pancake, I'll get you some of the real coffee." she said.

She took a sip of her coffee slowly. A small smile peeked out from around the rim of her mug.

"Wait, REAL coffee?" I asked. "Then what the heck is in these mugs?"

I could feel my eyes widening as I stared at her. Was it drugged? Some kind of weird hippy coffee substitute? I'd tried chicory once before and I was not a fan, to say the least.

"Decaf, of course. I already had some of the regular coffee when I went to talk to Mom." she said.

"DECAF?! Why the hell would you feed me decaf?!" I hissed.

"Well...It's all you had in your cabin's pantry. So when I made a pot in here, that's what I used. Also, the book says caffeine can dehydrate you and make your heat worse." she said, taking a bite of her pancake like she hadn't just confessed to a crime worse than murder.

"I'm going to kill you. I'm actually going to kill you." I said.

I couldn't get over the audacity of it. What kind of sick, evil sadist was she? I'd been all wrong about her maybe possibly being a rare good alpha.

She pouted at that. How could the devil be so cute? I made myself count backwards from ten. Can't lose my cool. "Omega in heat murders idiot alpha!" is the kind of headline that could set back omega rights in this country for a decade.

"Jessica," I said very slowly, "I usually have several cups of coffee a day. Now, do you know what happens when someone who regularly consumes caffeine does not get their caffeine?"

"Ooh, I know this one! They get a headache, and irritability and—oh." her excited voice trailed off as she made the connection.

"I'm sorry Summer. I just really wanted to motivate you to try to eat a little. It's supposed to help. Heats take a lot of energy so if an omega isn't taking in any calories, it drains their body even more." she said.

She was leaning forward over the tabletop, looking at me with an earnest expression.

I sighed. She seemed so well-intentioned, it was hard to stay mad at her.

"It's fine Jessica. I mean not really but...You need to learn to take my word on these things." I said.

She wilted back into her seat, looking up at me with wide woeful eyes.

"I promise I'll do better. I just want to help you as much as I can. And maybe that means listening to you more instead of digging up expert advice." she said.

"Yeah. Unfortunately a lot of the 'expert advice' is bullshit when it comes to omegas." I said. "But hey, I'm not saying they have it all wrong. They could be right about the food and caffeine thing. The implementation though...that was terrible." I said.

Jessica deflated even more, if that was possible. "That's my bad...the book just said you should help motivate your omegas to eat."

"Well don't start planning your career as a life coach or a motivational speaker," I said, smiling at the idea of weird, introverted Jess in such a charisma-based profession. "But I'll make a compromise with you."

She perked up, eyes alight with curiosity as she looked at me.

"What did you have in mind?" she asked.

"First, you give me some real coffee. That's your end of the bargain." I said.

She nodded.

"Now, for my part of the deal. I usually drink my coffee black. No sugar, no creamer or milk. But! Just in case your little book and its advice on calories is right, I'll let you add some creamer to my coffee this time, and only this time." I said.

"That's perfect! The heavy cream Dad uses in his coffee is like fifty calories per tablespoon, or something ridiculous like that." she said.

"See, this is why you need to listen to me. I'm full of great ideas." I said.

"You really are." Jessica said, without a trace of irony.

It was a struggle not to bury my face in my hands. This alpha really was too much.

***

Jessica left the cabin, and returned a few minutes later with a very large coffee cup, steam wafting off of the liquid in it. I eyed it greedily. I had abandoned the sad mug full of decaf coffee the moment I was told it was a fake, and it sat pathetic and half-full on the table.

I had eyes only for the real thing, and took the hot mug from Jessica's hands. I looked down at it. Sweet caffeine! It was a shame the liquid was a pale brown color from all the creamer, instead of the deep inky black I preferred. Black as my soul.

"I brought some of the sugar packets in case you decided you wanted some." Jessica said, dropping a few pink and blue packets on the table in front of me.

I squinted at them. Normally I don't add any sweetener, but since this thing was practically a damn coffee milkshake at this point, I suppose I might as well.

I emptied one of the packets into the coffee. Jessica sat down across from me, and picked up my plate.

"Sure you don't want this?" she asked.

I shook my head.

"Okay. If you change your mind, I can always make you another one." she said.

She began digging into the pancake with gusto. I focused on my coffee, sipping it slowly.

I ignored the growing urge to gulp it. The desire for it surprised me, because I always savor my first cup of the day. Maybe my heat really was making my body crave more calories. Still, I didn't trust it with anything solid. My body was always ready to disappoint me.

"So, what do you want to do for the rest of the day?" I asked.

I knew Jessica had promised to spend my heat with me, but I had a hard time believing she would stick to my side all day. Not because she's selfish or meant to lie, but because it was a beautiful day and she was on vacation.

I could hear the birds chirping outside, see the warm sunlight beaming through the windows—it was tempting *me* to go out, and I felt like living death and had every reason to hide inside.

Why would anyone stay cooped up inside with

a moping omega, when they could be out there hiking the trails or swimming in the river?

"It's really up to you Summer. We don't have to do anything at all. We can just sit around and chill, watch TV if you're up to it. Or I can bring over my books if you'd like to read." she said.

She paused, as if something had occurred to her.

"Or..." she trailed off with a coy little smile on her face.

"Or what?" I asked.

What could an alpha want to do with an omega that they would be so hesitant to fess up to? It had better not be anything lewd. She didn't seem like the type, but you never knew with alphas. You can't trust them.

"Or, I have some board games I brought along." she said.

There was a light blush dusting her cheeks now and she looked down at the plate in front of her.

Why did that suggestion have her looking so embarrassed? Of all the things she could've suggested, that was pretty innocent.

And it wasn't a bad idea either, when you considered how much my senses had heightened to an annoying extreme. Noise, light, movement could trigger pain, but sitting around playing with some pieces of plastic and cardboard cards was unlikely to harm anything.

"That might be good." I said. "What do you have?"

"Well, our cabin has some of the classic old ones like *Monopoly* and *Clue*. But I also brought along *Castles of Insanity* from home." she said.

"Are you kidding? I freaking love *Castles of Insanity*." I said.

"Really?" She looked up from her plate, smiling.

"Dude, it's me. I love spooky shit. You should see me on Halloween." I said. "Plus it's just fun."

"Try telling that to Aidan. I can never get him to play it. He says board games are for little kids." Jessica said, sighing.

"I have tried to tell him. And tried to get him to join my biweekly game of *Necromancer: thé Dansant*. He never will. I hate to say it Jessica, because he's my best friend, but...Your brother is a total normie." I said.

Jessica laughed. The sound brought a smile to my face.

"Maybe when this is over we can gang up on him and make him nerd out with us." Jessica said.

"Hell yeah." I said. "Through our forces combined, he won't stand a chance."

I held out my hand for her to fist bump. She stared at it with a perplexed look, long enough for the moment to become awkward. I was just about to drop my hand, feeling like an idiot, when she tentatively reached up and touched her knuckles to mine.

I hoped that her offer was genuine. When I'd started out on this trip, I never would have guessed Jessica was someone I would want to spend more time with, or would ever want to know better.

But now I was starting to think she really wasn't bad at all (for an alpha). It would be nice if she meant what she said, and we really would play games together in the future, even once this trip was over.

***

Jessica fetched Castles of Insanity, and we unpacked the game pieces and spread the board game out on the coffee table in the living room. We both sat on the floor to play.

We had both agreed to run two characters apiece, since the game was more fun with more characters in the running. But before we started, Jessica paused, hesitating.

"Hey, you need to pick out your characters." I prodded.

"Uhh..." she said.

"What is it?" I asked.

"Well..." she said.

Irritation rose up in me. "Come on, spit it out." I said.

Jessica seemed to operate in only two modes: overly confident and rambling enthusiastically, or quiet and walking on eggshells.

"Shouldn't we be touching? You know, to maximize skin-to-skin contact?" she laughed nervously.

"Sure? That makes sense. No reason to be weird about it." I said.

She could have just said that, instead of making me draw it out from her. And yet butterflies were fluttering in my stomach at the prospect of touching her again. It was stupid—I'd touched her plenty last night when we were sharing a bed. Whatever she had in mind now was probably less intimate than that.

Why would I be nervous about touching her now? It had to be Jessica's fault. Her being weird about it was making me weird about it. It was contagious weirdness.

Anxiety often doesn't last long for me; it makes me angry, which then pushes the anxiety down and prompts me to take action.

I thrust my left hand around the table toward her.

"Here, just hold my hand. We'll only need one hand free to move the game pieces. This way, we can stay touching." I said.

Blushing hotly, she took my hand. Her fingers were long and slender, cool against my skin where they intertwined with mine. I chose to ignore the awkwardness, and get started with the game.

After a few minutes, my attempts to play it cool and act normally paid off. Phony nonchalance morphed into genuine calm as we both got swept up in the game's story and forgot the oddness of our situation.

CHAPTER 7: SUMMER

We got so into our *Castles of Insanity* game that several hours flew by without us noticing. We had just slain a Lovecraftian horror and were high-fiving over it when a harsh rapping at the door broke the spell we were in.

Normally I would have cracked a joke about one of the horrors from beyond showing up at my cabin door to take revenge for us destroying its monstrous sibling-in-arms, but my throat was closing up.

Pulled out of my focus on the game, I was acutely aware again that I was an omega in heat, shacked up with an alpha I wasn't related to or mated to. And that we were trying to hide that fact from everyone except for Aidan.

What if it was Jessica's parents out there, or the campground manager? I wasn't sure which would be worse. My palms began to sweat.

"I'll get it. Just stay here." Jessica whispered.

Stay here? I felt like a mouse that had just been spotted by a large, hungry cat. My instincts screamed for me to flee to the nearest bolthole, but I knew Jess was right and it wouldn't do anything but make the situation look odder to whoever was out there.

Jessica stood up, her hand pulling free from mine. I instantly wanted it back. I craved the comfort of it, the feeling of security it brought, like she had a hold of me and I was under her protection.

I sat there frozen, watching as she walked away and opened the door. What I saw on the other side of the doorway vindicated my fear. The woman standing there was a tall brunette alpha, just like Jessica but older. Jessica's mom. I would rather have had Cthulhu knock at our door.

"Hi girls! Is everything alright?" Jessica's mom asked.

Her voice was cheerful, but her eyes were sharp as she looked over Jessica's shoulder and scanned the inside of the cabin.

I made myself give a little wave to Jessica's mom, and did my best to not flinch away from the harsh bright light of the sun that was pouring through the open door.

"Yeah Mom, we're all good here. We were just playing some board games," Jessica said. "I thought your hike today was an all-day one?"

Jessica's mom sighed, her face falling. "Your father forgot his medication, so we had to come back. We're going to get back on the trail in a bit. I think we can still finish the hike if we really hustle, and make it back before nightfall."

"That's good." Jessica said.

She didn't move away from the doorway. It made me feel a little better, to see her blocking the entrance. Even though I knew that made no sense, that Jessica's mom wasn't a physical danger. The threat she posed was all modern, the ability to fuck my life over with a few deductions, a few words.

"Summer honey, are you okay? The kids said you weren't feeling well." Jessica's mom asked, eyeing me.

"Yeah I'm fine Mrs. Hartwell. Just really beat from all that rowing yesterday. I'm not used to so much exercise." I said.

I may have hated the "omegas are physically weak and delicate" stereotype I was playing into, but I didn't hesitate to use it for furthering the greater good aka: me not getting in deep shit with my parents and getting sent home early from this vacation.

"Alright, if you're sure. Don't hesitate to ask me or Jim for anything, okay?" she said.

Jim was Jessica and Aidan's dad. I wasn't going to ask either of them for anything, but if I was going to, it would be Jim, not her, that I'd turn to for help. It's not because he's an omega and she's an alpha either. He was a lot more approachable than her.

But I just nodded to her. I didn't want to say more, because I didn't trust my voice not to quaver. I was sweating bullets now, afraid that at any moment she would catch a whiff of my scent and realize I was in heat.

Jessica had kept all of the windows in the cabin opened a crack, with the air conditioning going full blast and a box fan turned up to high for good measure, all to keep the air circulating well so my scent wouldn't pool too strongly inside and around the cabin.

She'd also put up several air fresheners, one in each room. I hated the artificial smell of them, but I knew I needed all the help I could get in covering up my scent.

All of these measures must have worked, because Jessica's mom turned around and left without saying another word. When Jessica closed the door, I slumped over the table in relief. It felt like an anvil's weight of pressure had been taken off my shoulders.

"That was close." Jessica remarked.

"How reassuring." I said.

"I'm not trying to stress you out. But my mom is really sharp. It's like she has a sixth sense for any kind of shenanigans." Jessica said.

"Still not helping!" I said.

I'd heard Aidan say the same thing about their mom before, and going off the suspicious way she'd examined the inside of the cabin, they weren't wrong. I did not like to think that she was already onto me.

"Alright, I'll shut up. Let's just get back to the game." Jessica said.

That I could agree with. Without prompting, she took my hand again, giving it a little squeeze of reassurance. I hated to admit it helped, but it did make me feel a little better. Still, my body felt weak all of a sudden.

"When we're done with this session, can we take a nap?" I asked.

Please say yes Jessica. Don't tell me it's the middle of the day, or that it's fine for me to take a nap, but you'll stay up and read.

 I needed the comfort and safety of my bed after that confrontation, and while I cursed the desire for it, I wanted the security of Jessica's arms around me. Stupid heat. Stupid Jessica's mom, scaring the crap out of me.

Jessica raised her eyebrows, but said, "Sure, that's probably a good idea."

I couldn't hold back my sigh of relief. I sounded sad

and pathetic even to my own ears.

"Don't worry Summer, you'll get through this." she said.

I hoped so. I really did. This heat had only been on for a day and already it felt like it had lasted forever.

***

The cabin's bed was comfortable. It had two fluffy soft pillows, a thick downy comforter, and the air conditioner nearby blew hard and cold, so that the air was pleasantly cool and wasn't stifling to be in bed on a hot summer day.

My limbs were entangled with an attractive alpha's, her lean muscular legs resting against my short slim ones. Her arm was thrown over my side, and mine was wrapped around her torso. We were so close our foreheads almost pressed together.

In the past, it would have put me on edge to have someone so far up in my personal space. But Jessica's nearness didn't bother me, if anything it was a comfort.

I felt safe, I was in a comfy spot, and my body was drained of energy. So why couldn't I sleep? My mind kept buzzing like it was on batteries.

Finally I gave up on falling asleep and opened my eyes.

"Jess?" I whispered.

Her eyes were closed and her breathing was deep and even. If she'd managed to fall asleep, I wasn't going to wake her just because I was feeling bored and antsy.

But her eyes opened at my voice, staring into mine. They seemed darker in the shadowed room, the blue seeming to hold all the depths of the ocean.

"What is it?" Jessica asked.

"I can't sleep." I said.

It sounded pathetic, but I couldn't help it.

Jessica pushed herself up onto her elbow.

"Do you want to head back into the living room and do something?" she asked.

I shook my head. There wasn't any better options for passing the time out there. I couldn't watch TV, and we'd played enough *Castles of Insanity* for me to be burned out on the game for awhile.

"Okay..." Jessica said, trailing off. She had her thinking face on.

"I'm too tired to do anything," I said, irritated. "Isn't there anything else that can speed this along? I'm sick of being in heat!"

Jessica chewed on her lip. "Not really." she said.

"'Not really?' That's not a 'no'." I said.

My question had been more of a complaint than a real request. After all, if there was anything useful we could do, she would have offered it up from the start, right? But now she was acting so hesitant to just say "Nope, sorry!" that I was sure she was hiding something.

"We-ell..." she said.

My temper spiked, anger coiling in my belly hot and burning. I pushed it down, keeping it under control.

"Tell me." I said.

"You're not going to like what I have to say. The studies on this were very inconsistent and inconclusive—" Jessica said.

"Jessica." I said, my voice coming out louder and sharper than I would have liked.

"Alright. A few studies indicated that maybe, perhaps, exchanging some body fluids can help accelerate the heat process." Jessica said.

"Of course," I said, "It couldn't be something normal like eating chocolate or doing a special yoga pose or something."

I shook my head. Nope, my body would never let me off that easy.

"So, what kind of body fluids are we talking about here?" I asked. "Blood, tears, or...?"

I didn't need to say that last one. We both knew.

"The studies were done on saliva, actually." Jessica

said.

"Spit? That's not so bad." I said.

There were so many worse options. I thought hard. I couldn't ask her to do it. Could I? It was just a kiss after all, one measly little kiss. It seemed like a small sacrifice to make to maybe speed up this whole intolerable ordeal.

"Would you?" I asked.

"What?" Jessica recoiled, shrinking a few inches back from me, as if she expected me to pounce on her. Her face was turning bright red.

"Would you kiss me?" I asked. "It doesn't have to be a big deal. Just a quick kiss." I wheedled.

"I can't kiss you!" she said. "You're my little brother's best friend a-and it would be taking advantage of you!"

I rolled my eyes. "Don't start with the helpless little omega crap," I said, "I'm asking you to slip me a little tongue, not form a life bond."

I didn't think it was possible for Jessica to turn any redder, but she did. Her skin was practically glowing with heat.

"Summer...I don't think you know what you're asking. I've never kissed anyone before. I'm completely inexperienced at that." she said.

"Pfft, no way." I said.

Jessica might be an awkward nerd at times, but she's still really good-looking. She was tall and slim with an athletic build, gorgeous wavy thick chestnut hair and strong but refined features. She was a babe!

And she was an alpha with chill parents. I knew they had never locked her up like a princess in a tower like I'd been. She's really trying to tell me she's never got as far as kissing someone?

This had to be a lame attempt to shake me off.

"Yes, way." Jessica said.

"How? Why?" I asked.

Maybe it was rude, but if she was telling the truth, I wanted all the details to this mystery. She was the kind of alpha girl who should have been beating off suitors with a stick, so what gives?

"It's not that complicated. I never had much time to date. I've always been too busy, with studying and sports and yearbook and chess club and—well you get the idea. Besides, no one has ever been interested in me." she said.

She looked down at the floor.

"Oh bullshit," I said, "I bet you're one of those people who is completely oblivious to people flirting with them."

Jessica shrugged. "It doesn't matter why, but it's the truth. I've never kissed anyone before and I wouldn't know where to start with you. I'm sorry Summer."

I sighed. I couldn't fault her for nerves or for not being up for a casual kiss if what she was saying was true, but there had to be some way around this. I buried my face in the pillow for a few moments, thinking.

Then I sat back up. "Aha!" I said.

I had to have some of her saliva, right? But there was nothing saying it had to be a kiss.

"Yeah?" Jess asked.

She was watching me warily.

"You don't have to kiss me. Just spit in my mouth." I said.

"WHAT?" she yelled.

"You heard me, spit in my mouth." I opened my mouth up wide and pointed a finger at my tongue.

"Oh my God, why?!" she wailed.

I started laughing.

"I want your saliva in me." I said, only half joking.

"That's so nasty, eww." Jessica said, she'd closed her eyes and scrunched up her face. She looked pretty adorable like that.

"Hey, there's always the traditional method of swapping spit." I said. "But this way, you wouldn't have to do something you're not ready for yet."

"I'm not going to spit in your mouth." she said, eyeing me like I was some kind of poisonous snake. "As for the kiss..."

"If it helps, I've only been kissed like once." I offered up, "and she wasn't very good at it, so the bar is set very low."

She sighed. "All right. I'll do it."

Yes! One step closer to ending this hideous heat.

I scooted closer to Jessica, our faces once more only inches apart. She was biting her lip again.

"Just relax. This is supposed to be enjoyable." I said.

Her nervousness set me at ease a bit. Maybe because it made me feel less like prey being pursued. Even with my sheltered existence, I'd dealt with way too many overconfident aggressive alphas trying to put a move on me. Jessica came across as the exact opposite of that.

There were still butterflies flapping their wings like mad in my stomach, but my body also buzzed with a pleasant energy that spurred me on.

I settled my arm over her body, and began closing in the gap between our faces centimeter by centimeter. My heart pounded. I was really doing this, I was going to kiss Jessica. I was almost dizzy with anticipation. I could hardly believe I was going to kiss an alpha I was in bed with—a hot older alpha at that.

Finally the moment of truth happened and my lips made contact with hers, brushing against them ever so lightly. Hers were soft and velvety like the petals of a rose, inviting one to touch and stroke.

I knew from my very limited kissing experience that having someone dive right in and shove their sloppy wet tongue deep into your mouth wasn't a good time. So I let our lips rest against each other for a moment, just enjoying the soft pressure of our mouths pressing together.

Jessica made a little noise, a sort of thoughtful hmm that sounded surprised and pleased. She grasped my shoulder and squeezed.

I took that as a sign of encouragement, and decided we were good to continue on. I just barely touched her lips with the tip of my tongue, and she parted them slightly. I slowly deepened the kiss, hyperaware of our breathing.

Everything seemed magnified, stronger, from the rough cotton texture of the sheets to the soft warm feeling of her skin against mine. Even Jessica's alpha scent, which I was always subconsciously aware of, seemed stronger. She smelled like an evergreen forest, not in a cheap car air-freshener way, but the clean healthy natural scent of real pine and cedar trees.

I'd started out tentative and slow, but with every second that passed without any sign of discomfort from her, I grew bolder.

She let me lead things, which didn't surprise me. I could practically picture the cogs in her mind turning, as she cataloged and considered this new experience she'd been so nervous about at first. She wasn't holding back so much as taking it all in.

But finally she pulled herself out of her contemplative state and took decisive action, darting her tongue out to swipe aggressively against mine. It sent an electric shock through me, a thrill of anticipation.

Our bodies pressed together closer, hands grasping as we continued to kiss and explore each other's mouths. Our tongues chased each other endlessly, an enthralling dance that should've gotten tiresome, but didn't.

I know I'd only asked her for a kiss, but I couldn't help letting it turn into more.

Jessica didn't protest when I ground down against her thigh, the harsh pressure pushing against my oversensitive mound enough to make me whimper into her mouth. It felt good though, and I kept it up.

The pleasure pooled hot and fast in my groin and I began to feel like I was drowning in the feeling. How could something so simple feel so good? It had to be the heat making me so responsive to any stimulation.

I was getting embarrassingly wet down there, and

my face flushed at the thought of Jessica realizing what a soaking mess she was making me.

She broke the kiss, and met my eyes.

"We should probably stop," she said, "that should be enough saliva I think."

"Y-yeah." I mumbled.

I didn't really want to stop. My body felt warm and pleased, like something hungry that had begun to get its fill. I couldn't think of a reason to push for us to continue. In fact, it shouldn't have gone as far as it did.

That thought didn't shut down the desire I had to wrap myself around her and never let go. What the hell had come over me?

I had pushed her to do this in the first place and then pushed it past what was reasonable for our agreement. When I looked at Jessica though, she had a reassuring smile on her face, lacking any anger or disgust.

Just because she didn't blame me didn't mean what I'd done was right. I looked away from her. I wasn't ashamed of kissing an alpha, but of taking advantage of a nice alpha's kindness to me? That was shitty.

Jessica had only agreed to hang out with me for a couple days to help me through my heat, and then I'd talked her into kissing me and acted like the worst stereotypes of an omega in heat. Shameless, throwing themselves at any alpha who would have them.

I didn't even realize I was crying, until one of her fingers swiped across my cheek, wiping away a tear.

"Hey, shhh. You didn't do anything wrong." Jess said.

"I'm sorry." I said.

I could feel my lips trembling around the words. I must have looked completely pathetic, but that was the least of my concerns at the moment.

"I'm serious Summer. You have nothing to be sorry for. That was a hell of a kiss, it was really nice." Jessica said.

"I didn't mean to get caught up in the moment. It must be because..."

Because what? Because I was in heat? It was lame as an excuse and if it wasn't an excuse but the truth, then that was even worse.

But whatever explanation I would've came up with for my behavior, I didn't get to share. Jessica shook her head.

"Don't worry about it." she said, patting my shoulder.

She seemed to genuinely not mind what happened. But I did. My skin was crawling with embarrassment from how I'd overstepped.

"Why don't we go into the kitchen and have something to eat? Or drink, in your case, if you still don't feel like eating. And then we could watch some TV with the volume turned down low. I think I know how to adjust the brightness on it too." Jessica said.

I could only nod. Her attitude on this was probably the best one to have. Move on, don't dwell on it, pretend it didn't happen and act normal.

If she was willing to let the kiss be swept under the rug, then I should do my part and leave it there. And hope she wouldn't later hold a grudge against me for taking things way too far with someone who wasn't interested.

She climbed out of bed, and I carefully followed her into the kitchen. She poured me a glass of water and loaded it up with ice cubes, and then set to work making sandwiches. I leaned against the counter and watched her. Mine was just cheese and a little lettuce.

Normally I would've rejected it, not because I have anything against cheese sandwiches but because of my appetite still being completely destroyed by my heat. But I felt so bad over the kiss that I went ahead and took it from her.

I sat across from her at the little table and nibbled at it slowly, only able to make myself eat half of the small sandwich.

When we were finished, we headed into the living room and I sat on the couch silently as she tinkered with the TV. Once she had it adjusted, we sat and watched the dimmed, barely audible TV for the next couple of hours.

CHAPTER 8: JESSICA

Keeping my mouth shut while we watched television was one of the hardest things I'd ever done. After what we'd done in the bedroom, I felt like a soda bottle that had been all shaken up and was ready to explode if someone took the cap off. If I let myself open my mouth, I'd have an absolute torrent of words to spill out.

I'd just had my first kiss and it had been *amazing*. Summer had been amazing. I'd opened my eyes several times during the kiss (were you supposed to keep your eyes closed during a kiss? Or was open okay? The sheer closeness to another person's face seems like it could make you go cross eyed...).

Whether it was how you were supposed to do it or not, I was glad I'd peeked. Summer had been so beautiful, her pale porcelain skin flushed delicately with heat, long dark lashes fluttering as she moved, her lithe little body graceful as it twisted against mine.

I wanted to talk to her about it and go over it

all a million times. Just verify that it had really happened, and hadn't been a wild dream, the unsurprising result of dozing off curled up in the arms of an omega in heat. But even I could tell that Summer wasn't in the mood to chat. She said she'd gotten more carried away then she'd expected, "caught up in the moment" and seemed upset over it.

Was it simply embarrassment at passionately kissing her best friend's older sister? Or was it because it was me, specifically? Gawky, awkward Jessica Hartwell, an annoying know-it-all that was utterly beneath a cute, confident omega like her?

Maybe that was my own self-esteem issues talking though. It was hard to be objective, but it was possible it had nothing to do with me at all, and was all about the actions alone. If she was telling the truth, she was very lacking in experience for such an attractive omega.

Maybe she had a general problem with sexual shame holding her back. There were many people that had hang-ups around normal desire and bodily gratification.

If so, it was none of my business. I wasn't her partner, despite us kissing. She'd gotten what she wanted from me, the saliva that could help speed up her heat. Her feelings on the matter were her own, she could share them with me if she wanted, but I wasn't going to pry where I had no right.

So I kept my lips zipped and we sat in silence watching old sitcoms for hours. I did get up the nerve to take her hand in mine (touch helped with the heat process! that was all!) and she let me hold it while we sat on the couch together. I let out a breath I didn't know I was holding when she didn't pull it away. She couldn't be too disgusted by me if she was holding my hand, right?

An awkwardness seemed to linger around us, the silence uncomfortably weighted with tension. It was a relief when someone knocked at the door. Summer startled a little, but I wasn't surprised. It had to be near dinner time, and someone had probably come to fetch us.

I gave Summer's hand a reassuring squeeze before unthreading my fingers from hers. Then I stood and went to answer the door.

My brother was on the other side of it. He probably volunteered to get us, to keep Mom and Dad from approaching the cabin and interacting with Summer any more than necessary.

Aidan stepped into the cabin, closing the door behind him. He saw Summer's face, and didn't say a word. He just crossed over to the couch and folded her into a hug. I fidgeted, not sure if I should sit back down or stay near the door to avoid intruding on their moment.

"That bad huh?" Aidan said.

"Not anymore than usual," Summer said, "I just can't wait for this to be over."

"Well, hopefully you two have been canoodling enough to speed things along." Aidan said.

Summer blushed, and I could feel my own cheeks heating up.

"Geez, I was joking. You two didn't actually do anything did you...?" Aidan asked.

"Shut up!" Summer said, and threw one of the couch pillows at him.

He caught it with ease and hid it behind his back so she couldn't nail him with it again. I laughed. Some of the tension in the air faded away.

"If we did, would you really want to know?" I asked.

"Good point. The less I know about my sister's love life, the better." Aidan.

"The feeling is mutual Aidan." I said wryly.

Unfortunately I'd had to hear a lot more about my brother's romantic ups and downs and escapades than he ever had to hear of mine. It seemed like every month there was a new girlfriend or boyfriend of his, or some heartbreaking unrequited crush he was mooning over (although he seemed to get over them awful fast...). Meanwhile my romantic history was nonexistent.

I opened my mouth to point that out, then closed

it. 'I have no love life, unlike you!' would probably be more of a self-own than the put-down of Aidan I intended it to be.

Before I could say anything else, we heard Mom's voice calling from outside, "Kids! Dinner!"

"We'd better get going before she comes in here." Aidan said, rising from the couch.

"I'll bring you back some leftovers, okay Summer? I know you probably won't want them, but they'll be there in the fridge in case you do." I said.

She nodded. "Thanks Jess."

Her eyes were dark and pensive looking up at me.

I hated leaving her behind, to suffer in isolation while the rest of us ate dinner, but I had to go out there or it would look even more suspicious.

And so I turned my back on her and followed Aidan out of the cabin, closing the door softly behind me.

***

Outside, Dad was once more manning the grill to ensure there would be pounds of and pounds of semi-charred meat to eat for dinner. Just like the night before. At this rate, by the end of the vacation I'd be ready to embrace vegetarianism like Summer.

Mom was setting down the plates and cutlery on the picnic table, which was already holding a large bowl of salad and a few bowls of other side dishes.

"Where's Summer?" Mom asked.

"She's eating in her cabin tonight. Said she doesn't like seeing and smelling meat." Aidan said.

"I could bring her over some of the salad—" Mom said.

"Don't worry about her, she has some vegetarian food she brought." I added.

Mom pursed her lips but said nothing.

I fetched a hamburger from Dad and loaded up my plate with food, and sat down at the picnic table with my family.

For the first couple minutes, we were too busy stuffing our faces to talk much. But before long Mom, Dad, and Aidan were filling me in on all the things I'd missed by not joining them on their hike earlier.

"Seems like the sort of thing you would've enjoyed Jessica." Mom said.

She watched my face closely as she waited for my answer. What was I, a bug under a microscope? I knew I could pass her scrutiny though. I have a naturally inexpressive face that doesn't easily show a lot of emotion.

It's not that I don't feel strongly about things. I think I just get so caught up in thinking about whatever I'm responding to, that my brain seems to forget to relay the message to my body.

I took a sip of my lemonade while I thought of what to say to her. "Probably, but I don't have to hike every trail. That wouldn't even be possible. I always have to save a few for the next trip."

"So, will you be joining us for tomorrow's hike?" she asked.

"Come with us Jess, you can't spend the whole week indoors. Misses the whole point!" Dad chimed in.

I cast him a quick smile. Dad's enthusiasm at least, was genuine and without any ulterior motive.

"Don't worry, I'm not going to miss out on hiking this time. We have a whole week. I can afford to take one day easy, hanging out with Summer while her muscles recover from the float. It's not good to overdo it with physical exertion when in heat."

Oh shit, what did I just say? Me and my big mouth.

"This heat I mean! The hot temperatures! What is it, ninety-five degrees?" I laughed, grabbing one of the spare paper plates and fanning myself with it, my movements a bit more frantic than they should have been.

"Usually you're the one champing at the bit to go everywhere and see everything on these trips." Mom said.

What was she fishing for? I'd spent one day

121

hanging out with Summer in her cabin. Did she have to be so suspicious? Sure, what we were up to was probably worse than anything she was suspecting, but still. Have some trust in your kids!

"I guess I've matured." I said piously.

Aidan laughed so hard he spat potato salad back onto his plate.

"Aidan! Ugh, gross." I said.

Mom just handed him a napkin.

"So, can we count on you to show up tomorrow?" Mom asked.

"Sure." I said.

I hoped so. I didn't know how long I could keep her off our back if Summer's heat continued much longer.

"And what about Summer?" Mom asked.

I shrugged. How was I supposed to know? Even if Summer wasn't in heat, it's not like I'd know whether she wanted to go on the hike or not.

Aidan came to the rescue. "I don't know Mom. Summer has never been as outdoorsy as us. She's new to this sort of thing. She might be tired of it already. It wouldn't surprise me if she decided she doesn't like the heat and the bugs and just wants to get back to civilization as soon as possible." he said.

"Well I hope that's not the case." Mom said,

frowning.

"Nothing we can do on that front." Aidan said.

"Hey Dad," he said, changing the subject, "do you have that photo of that duck on your phone? Jess should see it."

I perked up. Who doesn't want to see cool birds? And it was a way less risky conversation topic then Summer or the hike.

"It wasn't a duck, Aidan. It was a heron—" Mom corrected.

I leaned forward to look at Dad's phone. Duck, heron, eagle, parakeet—I don't care. A cool bird is a cool bird, and all birds are cool.

The rest of dinner passed like that, with Aidan and I carefully avoiding any dangerous topics in favor of steering the conversation towards safer waters.

It was exhausting. I wasn't used to keeping secrets, having to always be alert to what I might blurt out that could incriminate myself. Aidan though, had always gotten into enough youthful hijinks for the both of us, and was well-versed in keeping Mom off the trail.

It was a relief when dinner was over. After cleaning everything up, we all started getting ready for bed. I'd have to sneak out to rejoin Summer, but at least I wouldn't have to worry about dodging any more questions from my parents.

Aidan and I took turns using the bathroom. Even though I wasn't really going to bed yet, I went through my normal nightly routine. All washed up and with a clean pair of pajamas on, I slid in beneath the covers.

It was boring just laying there, but I had to wait long enough for my parents to drift off to sleep. It wouldn't have been so bad if I had Summer in my bed; lying around doing nothing was easy when it was with her.

I had never thought I'd enjoy snuggling, I'm not a touchy-feely sort of person at all. Being snuggled up against her was peaceful though, calming and restful, enjoyable in some visceral way. I'd be experiencing that soon enough. I took a peek at my phone.

Finally, an hour had gone by. That had to be long enough, right? The average human falls asleep within twenty minutes of going to bed, and my parents had never complained of insomnia.

I climbed out of bed and padded to the bedroom door, turning the handle slowly and opening it just a few inches for me to slip through. The hallway was dark but there was nothing in it to trip me up.

When I made it into the living room, there was no sign of movement or life anywhere. I crept around the furniture, navigating by the dim light coming through the windows from the porch light outside. With one last look around the room to make sure I hadn't woken anyone, I slowly opened the front door.

I squeezed through the little bit I'd opened it, and then oh-so-slowly pulled it closed behind me, not making so much as a click. I let out a sigh. I'd made it! I allowed myself a small victory smirk.

I started towards Summer's cabin on bare feet, but I hadn't even made it off the porch when a voice spoke up from behind me.

"Out for a midnight stroll Jessie?" a deep baritone asked.

I leapt about a foot in the air, and spun around. I'd barely managed to keep from shrieking. It was a good thing I'd managed to keep my mouth shut, because if I'd cried out it would have brought Mom out as well.

My father was in the cabin's entrance way. He stepped out, closing the door quietly behind him. I watched him with trepidation as he settled down into one of the camp chairs that were sitting on the cement slab porch, but he didn't look angry. He had a small smile on his face.

What the heck was he doing up? Now that I thought about it, I hadn't heard his loud snoring as I made my way out of the cabin. Dad had a snore that could wake the dead. I should have noticed its absence.

'Stupid, Jess, stupid.' I cursed myself internally.

Meanwhile my father waited patiently for my answer.

"I'm just getting some air." I stammered out.

I could feel my heart rate increase under Dad's considering look.

"Hmmm." was all he said.

I swung my arms at my sides, shaking them a bit. Trying to burn off some of the adrenaline generated from getting caught in the act. Well, not quite. It could have been worse—Dad could have stepped out onto the porch as I was opening Summer's door.

Who says I'm not an optimist? I leaned against the cabin wall next to our front door, trying to look casual. Yup, nothing to see here, just cooling off in the summer night.

"I couldn't sleep," I said, "I think it's the noise from all the cicadas keeping me up. It's just so hard to tune them out, you know?"

I knew I should be keeping my mouth shut, volunteering nothing, certainly not rambling idiotically, but when had I ever had control over my mouth?

"Cicadas keeping you up? Or a certain omega?" Dad asked, the crows' feet at the corners of his eyes deepening along with his smile.

Dad's tone was light and teasing, it wasn't an

accusation. I relaxed a little. It was possible I could come out of this okay—if I played my cards right.

"I don't know what you're talking about." I said, not about to spill my guts that easily.

"Hey, I was young once. Your mom and me aren't so old that we've gone blind. We noticed how much time you've been spending with Summer. I guess you two really hit it off during the float?" Dad asked.

"Summer's cool," I admitted, "but we're just friends. Maybe not even that." I said.

There was a bitter pang in my chest. What I'd told Dad was the truth, unfortunately. A few days of being friendly with each other did mean we'd formed a lasting friendship, let alone anything more.

I wasn't sure Summer would want anything to do with me once her heat was over and I was no longer useful to her. Sure, we seemed like we'd hit it off somewhat while we were sharing a canoe, and we'd had a lot of fun playing board games together, but I couldn't rely on that to mean anything.

I'd had too many experiences in my life, where someone was happy to share my company when they needed a lunch table, or lab partner to do most of the work, or when we were the only people our age at some event our parents had dragged us to.

But the minute I was no longer useful or better options came along, someone more fun and cool, I was left in the dust. Tolerable enough when there was no one else, easy enough to get along with when brought together by circumstances, but missing something that made people want to be around me.

"Hey, if she can put up with your brother all these years I'm sure you've got nothing to worry about." Dad said.

"Thanks Dad." I said, resisting the urge to roll my eyes.

He wasn't right though, not even a little. Aidan was more likable than I could ever dream of being. If we were foods, he'd be something almost everyone liked, like pizza. Meanwhile, I was something only a few people would stomach — sauerkraut maybe, or liverwurst. I might have more achievements than my brother, but when people thought of fun, they didn't think of me.

"Don't sell yourself short kiddo. You're a catch and whoever snaps you up will be one lucky omega." Dad said.

"I'm pretty sure I'm going to die alone at this point." I said, my tone dry.

Dad laughed. "Well, I'm not going to stand in the way of your one shot at romance then. Why don't you go ahead and meet up with your omega?" he asked.

My face heated up. "She's not my omega!"

"But she could be." Dad said.

"Shouldn't you be telling me to go back to my room or warning me about the dangers of promiscuity or something?" I asked.

Dad shrugged his massive shoulders.

"You and Summer are both adults, even if you're young. You can make decisions for yourself. Now, if it was your brother out on this porch, I'd be giving a whole different speech. But I know I can trust you to keep a level head and be safe." he said.

"And what about Mom? I asked.

If there was a "cool parent" in our family, it was definitely Dad. Mom was the more strict one. If she was here, she would herd me back to my room and lecture me about being young and impulsive and not letting my hormones rule me and so on (and on and on). As if I had ever been the kind of person to be impulsive or act immaturely! Dad was right to trust me.

Hopefully helping Summer out wouldn't end up being my first experience in doing something Aidan-levels of dumb...

Dad was continuing on, "What your mother doesn't know won't hurt her. Just don't give me any reason to regret putting trust in you."

"Thanks Dad." I said.

I leaned over and gave him a quick hug. Then I started off towards Summer's cabin. Halfway there, I stopped and turned around. Dad was still sitting in his chair, looking up at the night sky.

I called over to him, keeping my voice as low as I could and still be heard. "I am not going to be doing anything romantic or uh, *adult*, with Summer. I am just keeping her company!" I said, pointing a finger at him for emphasis.

I wanted to get that straight, and not give Dad the wrong idea. I didn't need him thinking his daughter was headed for wedding bells and a mate bond any time soon.

Dad was a hopeless romantic and very family-oriented, exactly the kind of omega who couldn't wait to help plan his kids' weddings and would no doubt dote endlessly on his grandchildren (if I or Aidan had any).

Dad just laughed at my words, the sound of his rich hearty chuckle drifting across the lawn as I spun around and walked up to Summer's cabin. I tapped the front door softly with my knuckles, just barely making a sound.

Summer must've been waiting up for me, because the door flew open and a hand grabbed my wrist, pulling me inside. For someone with such dainty looking hands she was strong. I did not say that aloud, my one brain cell must've been functioning.

Inside Summer's cabin the living room lamp was still on. Once my eyes adjusted to the light, I could see her clearly. She was dressed for bed as well, in sleep shorts and a thin tank top.

The amused smile that had been on my face since my conversation with Dad slid right off when I saw her expression.

She looked more weary than I'd ever seen her (and I'd been around a couple times when her and Aidan pulled an all-nighter to stay up and play some video game they'd gotten at a midnight release until it was time for school the following morning.) The strain of the past two days had clearly caught up to her and taken its toll. The shadows under her eyes were purple, and her mouth was twisted in a stressed-out little frown.

I closed the door behind me, getting one last glimpse of Dad stargazing. I turned my attention back to Summer.

"Hey Summer, how are you feeling?" I asked.

"Let's see: every inch of my body aches, I'm exhausted no matter how much I rest, I haven't eaten properly in a day and a half, and I have to live in constant fear of being found out and sent home. How do you think I feel?" she asked.

"Sorry." I said, meaning it.

I really did feel bad for her. She was suffering so much from a biological function of her body that she couldn't control. Her experience seemed hellish enough without also having to keep it hidden because of society's bullshit. It wasn't fair that Summer couldn't just come and enjoy a simple stress-free vacation like everyone else.

Summer's face softened at my weak apology.

"It's not your fault. I'm just glad you're here now." she said.

I could feel myself practically glowing when she said that. It was nice to have someone want me around. Even if it was only temporary, until I outlived my usefulness.

"So, are you ready for bed?" I asked.

I was only a little sleepy myself, and could have easily stayed up for a few more hours, but Summer looked like she was about to fall over.

She nodded to me as she stifled a yawn.

"Yeah, I've been waiting for you to get here so I can finally go to bed. It's been hard staying awake." she said.

"Well, let's not waste any more time then. Come on." I said.

She followed me down the hall towards her bedroom. It was funny; at this point I was more familiar with her bedroom than I was with my own room back in my family's cabin.

The bedroom was just as I remembered it, my own strong alpha scent still lingering there, intermixed with Summer's overpowering sweetness. Evergreen trees and flowers. It was a good combination. I climbed into my side of the bed, and got under the covers.

Summer lingered next to the bed for a moment, just standing there. I watched her chest rise as she took a deep, slow breath. I raised a brow, curious. Was she nervous? But before I could ask, she'd let her breath out and climbed under the covers, sliding up next to me.

She wriggled til she was up against me, and I wrapped my arms around her, taking the big spoon position. I kept my grasp on her loose enough so that she could move freely, but let the weight of my arms rest on her so she could feel my presence even while asleep, and benefit from the skin-to-skin contact from our bare arms touching. The front of my legs nestled against the back of hers. She was so warm.

I sighed, a strange contentedness flowing through me. There was something deeply soothing in what we were doing. It felt right. Like I was meant to have an omega in my arms, someone to protect and take care of. Was this what the role of an alpha was really about? If so, I could finally understand why being an alpha was considered lucky. This was bliss.

Was it just because I was an alpha and she was an omega? Or was it because she was Summer, and I was falling for her? If so, I was falling hard.

I knew it could only end like all of my previous infatuations had, even the platonic ones. With me crashing down to the ground and back to reality, where the truth would sink in that the enthusiasm and interest wasn't mutual. But I was helpless to stop myself from getting hyped up over someone I thought was great. All I could do was enjoy it while I had it, and bask in the delusion that someone might like me back.

It wasn't pleasant to think about, so I put the whole mess from my mind and focused on the steady rise and fall of Summer's breathing. Lying next to her, I fell asleep quickly.

CHAPTER 9: JESSICA

I woke with a confused yelp, the shreds of my pleasant dreams flying away as I was yanked into wakefulness without any warning. There was a tremendous crash shaking the cabin. My heart was racing, but the white flash that went off outside the cabin window clued me into what was happening. The room was briefly illuminated.

I pressed my hand to my chest, making myself breathe slowly. It was just a thunderstorm, the one that I'd read about in the weather forecast. It was what had prompted me to bring the board games on the trip so we'd have something to do if we were stuck inside due to the rain.

I felt sweet vindication course through me. I had been right about the storm! And Aidan had been wrong when he called me an over-prepared nerd for packing books and board games for an outdoors vacation. I couldn't wait to say "I told you so!" to him.

But I was pulled from my triumphant inner

crowing when I felt Summer trembling against me. The storm must have woken her up too. I leaned over and switched the bedside lamp on.

"Summer?" I asked.

I didn't bother to keep my voice down. The sound of the rain pounding against the walls would cover up anything, even if my family had also been woken by the storm. Unless my parents thought to check up on me and Aidan in our bedrooms...I gulped. I might be in deep shit because of this storm.

But there was nothing I could do about that risk, so I let it go. Besides, I had Summer to take care of. She was still shaking and clinging to me.

"W-what the hell is happening?" she mumbled, rubbing at her eyes frantically.

I hated seeing her so scared.

"It's just a thunderstorm." I assured her.

"It sounds like the whole fucking cabin is going to blow away." she said, her dark eyes wide.

The wind was howling ferociously, whistling around the cabin walls. There had been no tornado risk reported in the forecast though, so I felt safe enough.

"It'll be okay. Let's try to get back to sleep." I said.

"Like anyone could sleep through that." Summer grumbled, but laid back down.

I left the lamp on so that the flashes of lightning wouldn't be so startling when they went off. And so if the thunder awoke her again it wouldn't be quite so frightening, waking up in a strange room in the dark.

I wrapped my arms around her once more, holding her more tightly this time. She seemed to welcome it, snuggling back against me. I ran one of my hands over her shoulder and down her side, then rubbing and patting her back soothingly.

Before long, her breathing slowed and I could tell she'd fallen back asleep. I didn't sleep though. I stayed awake and listened to the storm, and watched over the omega who had trusted me to help her and keep her safe. That trust felt as unbreakable as iron, as if I'd rather die than let her down.

It was such a strangely sentimental feeling, not rooted in logic at all. It should have bothered me, who liked facts and reasonable explanations for everything. But it didn't. I just let myself feel it and be content.

I stayed there like a silent sentinel, until the stormy night gave way to a calm warm dawn.

***

I didn't have to wait til noon for Summer to wake up for the day. Around eight in the morning, she stirred and stretched out all her limbs. When she sat up, I saw that she had terrible bed head, the pale silvery blonde strands tangled and sticking in every direction, like a bird's nest on her head.

"Looks like the storm did a number on your hair. Did you sneak out in the night without me noticing?" I joked.

There was no way that she could have, but I wasn't about to fess up to playing guard dog all night.

She blinked, and patted at her hair. "It just does this sometimes. My hair is like the rest of my body —always rebelling against me."

"You want my help combing it out?" I asked.

I'd never combed anyone else's hair, but it couldn't be that much harder than combing out your own, right? Besides, it would be nice to touch her hair. It always looked so silky.

"Maybe, hold on a sec—" Summer said.

She was frowning, her face scrunched up in concentration. I tensed up, ready to take action if there was something wrong with Summer. Was she experiencing a heat complication?

But after a minute, her face relaxed and a small smile formed, then bloomed into an enormous grin.

"Feeling better now?" I ventured.

"Yeah. Yeah, I am! I don't ache anywhere, and the light isn't hurting my eyes." Summer said, pointing at the bright sunlight streaming through the window.

"That's good." I said. I'd hated seeing her miserable, even if it was what had allowed me to spend time with her.

"Smell me." she demanded.

"Uhh...What?" I asked, nonplussed.

"Smell me. I don't think I'm in heat anymore!" she said, her voice bubbling with happiness.

Cautiously, I leaned toward her and sniffed the air around her. Summer did smell different this morning.

She was still carrying a floral scent, like fresh violets, but it was less heavy and rich. Instead it barely lingered near her, a soft and almost imperceptible hint of flowers. A person probably wouldn't notice it at all, unless they were very close or were actively trying to pick up her scent. It was the level of scent output one would expect from an omega going about their daily life, not that of an omega sequestered for heat.

"I think it's your normal scent." I said.

I didn't want to give her false hope if that wasn't the case; it's not like I'd spent a lot of time smelling Summer before this week. I had no idea if she went through fluctuations in scent strength during her heats. Or if she was like Dad, and this meant her heat was over.

Summer let out a squeal, a bright unabashedly joyous sound that I'd never heard from her before.

Without any warning, she threw her arms around me and pulled me in for a hug. Startled, I let out a little squeak and froze. I wasn't bothered, just surprised, but Summer abruptly released me.

Before she could apologize, I gave her a broad smile and interrupted her.

"Hey, congratulations. You made it." I said.

I had to be happy for her. I *was* happy for her, truly. Her misery and pain were over for this cycle. And she didn't have to be afraid of being found out and sent home now. She could enjoy her vacation and exploring the outdoors without worry.

But then why did I feel so upset? It felt oddly like sour grapes jealousy, like something had been stolen from me. Maybe the day we would have had together if her heat hadn't ended. But Summer hadn't robbed me of that, it wasn't something I was entitled to in the first place, especially at the expense of her happiness.

I knew it was completely inappropriate and selfish to feel disappointed that she would no longer need me around. But knowing that didn't make the feeling go away. Stupid feelings, always doing what they wanted instead of listening to our thoughts, which are so much more reasonable.

But she was probably going to spend the rest of the

vacation with *Aidan*, while I was left in the dust. Ugh!

Summer didn't pick up on the simmering acidic brew of emotions inside me. Having an inexpressive face and non-emoting scent really pays off sometimes.

She was positively beaming at me.

"Thanks Jess," she said, "I can't thank you enough for all your help."

I shrugged. "I'm not sure it made any difference."

"I think it did. I really don't think I would've made it through this without you." Summer said.

Now I felt even guiltier for not being one hundred percent happy for her. I pushed the feeling away. It wasn't time to stew in my own mopey feelings right now.

"Hey, I'm always happy to help." I told Summer. "Come on, let's get dressed so we can tell Aidan the good news."

He would also be able to verify that Summer's scent had indeed returned to normal, since he knew her regular scent much better than I did. The thought shouldn't have bothered me. I really needed to stamp this envy out quickly. Otherwise I was going to end up hurting even more.

We got dressed in our regular day clothes, a lightweight white t-shirt and tan cargo shorts for me (you never know when a "Who has the most pockets?" contest might spring up. And I always liked to be prepared when out in the woods.).

Summer's shorts were a deep red corduroy, and much shorter than mine, showing her legs off to advantage. Her white blouse was high-necked with a pleated front. Way too fancy to be tromping through the woods in, but it's not like she'd had a reason before to buy more rugged clothing. At least it was a sleeveless blouse and light in color, a pale shade of cream.

"Do you want to use the bathroom first or...?" I asked.

She shook her head and grabbed my arm, pulling me into the bathroom. Dumbfounded, I just looked at her. She unzipped a small travel bag that was sitting on the vanity, and pulled out a plastic pack. There were five toothbrushes in it, and she thrust one at my hand. I took it, looking it over.

"You brought spares?" I asked.

I hadn't.

"I always bring a whole set with me if I'm away from home. What would you do if you dropped your toothbrush while you were away?" Summer asked.

Wash it off? Was what I thought, but definitely didn't say aloud. I didn't want her to think I was gross.

She put toothpaste on her own brush, then handed me the tube.

"We can just brush at the same time, I don't want to have to wait any longer to get out there." she said, and started brushing.

With a bemused smile I started brushing too.

Summer was so happy it was infectious. Even while she was brushing her teeth she was grinning, and not just because she needed to run the brush over her teeth. I couldn't help but feel a little better seeing how pleased she was.

We finished up in the bathroom, and headed out of the cabin. My stomach was doing weird little flip-flops as we stepped onto the porch. I wasn't sure if it was my body bracing itself for my upcoming abandonment by Summer, or if it was my apprehension about whether her heat was really completely over or not.

What if we stepped out there and it wasn't okay? And Mom or Dad pointed their finger at Summer and said "Aha! She's in heat! Get thee to a nunnery!"

Okay, maybe not that, but the modern equivalent.

I looked around the campground. It was nice out now—depending on your definition of nice. There wasn't a cloud in the sky, nothing to shield the water-logged earth from the sun's hot rays. The ground was practically steaming out its excess humidity. I wrinkled my nose at how muggy it was.

Everyone else was already outside, Mom and Dad busy getting breakfast ready, and Aidan was slumped over the picnic table looking only half-awake. Maybe that's why Mom noticed us first.

She cast a glance over at Summer's cabin when the screen door banged shut behind us. Mom did a double-take when she saw me arm-in-arm with Summer, her eyes practically bugging out of her head.

I did my best to ignore it. Summer was already pulling me over to where Aidan was sitting. My brother's eyes widened when he spotted Summer as well, but after taking a delicate sniff of the air, he relaxed.

"I see you made it out to the other side." Aidan said.

"Yep! Summer one, biology zero." Summer crowed.

"Finally. It was getting boring hanging out with Mom and Dad all the time." Aidan said.

"Aw, did you miss me little brother?" I asked.

He held his hand out, tilting it from side to side. "Eh, I can take or leave you. It's Summer I needed."

A pang shot through me at his words, even though I knew he was just teasing. Usually the "ugh lame big sister" type jokes didn't bother me, but sometimes the ribbing hurt. Only when I was already feeling especially sensitive about being disliked though.

I didn't have time to suffer my insecurities though, because my mother interrupted.

"Breakfast is ready! Come and get it before it gets cold!" Mom called.

Like anything was getting cold today. It had to be ninety degrees out already. You could probably fry an egg on the concrete porch.

I glanced over my shoulder at her.

"In a second Mom!" I called out.

Lowering my voice, I asked Aidan, "So she does smell okay?"

Aidan's face sank, and he lowered his eyes dramatically to the ground.

"No worse than she usually does." he said.

Summer pulled her arm free of mine to punch him on the arm. Aidan hissed.

"Is that how you treat a friend? Especially one who helped cover your ass… " he said.

"Yeah. And that favor is why I'm not kicking your ass." Summer said.

I rolled my eyes and stood up. I was hungry and whatever Mom had made us smelled good. I just hoped she wouldn't grill me before I got a chance to eat. No one should face an interrogation on an empty stomach. Aidan and Summer trailed behind me as I walked over to where Mom was filling up plates for us.

It looked like she was plating up breakfast burritos.

"Here you are. A ham, egg, and cheese one for Jessica and Aidan, and a tofu and cheese one for you Summer. I wasn't sure if you eat eggs or not..." Mom trailed off.

"Tofu is good." Summer said, taking the plate Mom held out to her.

We took our food back to the picnic table. Mom and Dad joined us a couple moments later. Aidan and I practically inhaled our burritos, but Summer ate more slowly. In the end she only finished half of her breakfast, but it was good to see her eating again.

When everyone was finished with their food, Mom turned to us.

"Will you be joining us on our hike today Summer?" Mom asked.

"I don't feel like walking a whole trail today," Summer said, "I thought I'd just wander around and do some mushroom hunting, if I can get these two to go with me."

"I'll go with you!" I blurted out, before I could think about it. I wanted to clap my hands over my mouth almost as soon as I said it.

'Don't come across as too eager, you know that weirds people out.' I chided myself.

My earnestness and over-enthusiasm for all kinds of different activities had been labeled as "totally and completely cringe" by Aidan years ago, and as far as I know he never revised that opinion.

But today everyone just took a brief glance at me, and then seemed to dismiss my weirdness (I guess they were all used to it at this point).

Aidan spoke up. "I'll go too. I could use a more relaxed day. We did what, twelve miles yesterday? My feet are killing me." he complained.

"Well I hope you kids won't just lounge around the campsite all week." Mom said, putting her hands on her hips.

I bit back a retort. We weren't kids anymore and if we wanted to lay around and do nothing for an entire week, we could. She couldn't make us anymore. Not that I had ever minded being dragged to whatever trail or cave or swimming hole Mom and Dad had picked out for the day. The fact that our preferences were so similar was one reason why family vacations usually went smoothly despite Mom's bossiness.

"Typical alphas, butting heads." Dad would always say, on the rare occasions I did get into a dispute with Mom.

It's bullshit, considering Aidan, who is a beta,

argues with her way more about all kinds of things. But today, he was playing peacemaker.

"Don't worry Mom, there's loads more stuff we want to do before the week is up." he said.

"Alright then." Mom said.

That was the end of that.

We cleaned up the campsite, putting away the leftovers and washing up the few dishes and utensils that weren't disposable. Then Mom and Dad left for their hike. Once they were out of sight, Aidan turned to Summer.

"You were just having her on right? You don't really want to go mushroom hunting or whatever, do you? What even is that?" Aidan asked.

I opened my mouth to explain mushroom hunting to Aidan, and then closed it. It had never occurred to me when Summer asked us to do it, that she might not have really wanted to look for mushrooms. Was it another one of those things that no normal person would want to do, so obviously it was an excuse? I had put my foot in it plenty of times by taking people's words straightforwardly, assuming they meant what they said.

I don't know why people so often say things they don't mean, when the truth would be so much easier and not bad at all, but that's how people are so I've just had to get used to it.

My eyes darted to Summer's face, trying to read her intentions. She still looked a little wan from getting over her heat, but she was smiling.

"Of course I want to go," Summer said, "And as for what mushroom hunting is...weren't you listening to me at all last semester when I told you about the mycology class I was taking?"

"No, never." Aidan answered, perfectly sincere.

"Well, you're about to get an entire semester's worth of ramblings packed into one day then. Prepare yourself for the mushroom education of a lifetime." Summer said.

"I should have went on the hike with Mom and Dad." Aidan groaned.

"Shut up and go fetch us some knives and wax paper from the kitchen." Summer ordered.

He headed towards our cabin, muttering "What the hell is wax paper?"

I laughed.

"I'm going to fetch my basket and the supplies I brought." Summer told me.

"Okay. Did you always plan on collecting mushrooms during this trip then?" I asked.

She shrugged.

"I wasn't sure if we'd get the chance. This isn't really the season for them. But with all the rain there was last night, a lot of mushrooms might've sprouted up. Just like you packed board games in case of rain, I packed my mushroom identification field guides." Summer said.

Field guides, plural. I couldn't help but smile at seeing Summer's own brand of nerdiness. I watched her as she walked back to our cabin, an odd flutter in my chest. I was on a tightrope wavering between nervousness and excitement.

Summer had invited me along for the day! She wanted to spend time with me even though she didn't need me anymore. That had to mean something, right? She could have just as easily ditched me to hang out with Aidan, if she really didn't want me around she could have just not invited me.

Unless it was just one of those invitations done out of politeness, that you're supposed to know to turn down because they don't really want you to accept? (But then why make the offer? Argh, it's so confusing!).

The thought chewed at me, that Summer's invitation was just done out of residual gratitude for the help I'd given her, and it would wear off quickly.

Still, I was being given another chance to spend time with her, another opportunity to impress her. I could be useful and interesting, right?

Now I just had to not screw things up...easier said than done if you're like me and seem addicted to misreading people and putting your foot in your mouth.

I didn't have long to brood over the unlikeliness of my success because Aidan and Summer returned with the items they'd went to collect. Aidan had even managed to find wax paper. I put my worries aside for now. It was a time for action, not introspection.

"Are you going to lead the way Summer? You probably know best where to look for mushrooms." I said.

"I didn't have any specific destination or path in mind. But sure, I can lead us in wandering aimlessly through the woods. Just keep in mind, I don't have much practical experience. So please stop me if I'm going to lead us into a ravine or a rattlesnake nest or something." Summer said.

"It would be a copperhead nest here." Aidan said, as we set off into the forest with Summer taking point.

"Now who's the know it all?" I teased him.

"Hey, I'm not going to get many opportunities to school Summer. It's only fair since she's going to torture us with a bunch of boring mushroom facts. I have to return the favor." Aidan said.

As we traipsed through the woods, Summer did

give us some mushroom facts. She seemed to know something about every toadstool or clump of lichen we came across. Aidan may have found it boring, but I listened raptly as Summer explained which ones were edible, and which ones were poisonous, and how to tell them apart.

It was fascinating to me how some of the mushrooms that looked nearly identical could have such opposite effects. One was a tasty bit of dinner, while its twin could kill you.

I soon found out why we brought knives when we came across a massive clump of fungus that Summer called "hen of the wood" growing at the base of an oak tree.

"Cut some of these off for me, will you Jessica?" Summer asked.

I knelt without question and began sawing away at the tough brown mushrooms.

"Putting the alpha to work?" Aidan asked. "You don't have to put up with that Jessica. Summer is supposedly an enlightened omega, she believes in sharing work out equally."

"If you want to make sure the work isn't all put on one person, then help your sister." Summer said, putting her hands on her hips.

"No way, I'm not enlightened. Jessica is stronger." Aidan said.

I ignored their bickering, concentrating on cutting

off a good amount of the mushrooms, without accidentally slicing myself.

After I'd freed some of the clump, Summer stopped me.

"That should be enough Jessica. We need to leave some for the other people or animals who might come along." Summer said.

I stood up with my bounty of mushrooms in hand, and passed them along to her to store in the basket.

Our trek resumed. It was pleasant, walking along with the others in quiet companionship. The sun was bright and its rays beat down on us through gaps in the tree canopy now and then, but most of the woods were lightly shaded.

There were all sorts of bugs and birds making a cacophony of sound. So many of them were buzzing or rubbing their wings together or singing, that you couldn't easily pick out individuals unless you saw them.

At one point we passed by a particularly thick old tree, the largest I'd ever seen. Its trunk was so massive that if the three of us tried to place our hands together to encircle the tree, we wouldn't have been able to link up.

There were other visuals the tree brought to mind though. It was a shame Aidan was here.

If I didn't have my brother around to cramp the

mood, it would have been the perfect place to lean a cute omega girl up against to kiss her senseless...

I thought of the way Summer's face had looked yesterday when she kissed me. That rosy blush on her cheeks, the serious, intense focus in her eyes when she leaned forward. I remembered how it felt to be on the receiving end of that laserlike gaze. It hadn't been bad. Thinking about it sent a little shiver through me despite the heated summer day. I rubbed my hands together, trying to dispel the weird frisson of energy pooling in me.

'Bad Jessica, you get those thoughts right out of your head. That's not ever going to happen again. She just needed your saliva because of her heat. She doesn't like you like that. You'll be lucky if she even wants you as a friend.' I mentally scolded myself.

That's right, even the so-called "friend zone" is a place I'd gladly occupy. I just want to keep spending time with her, to have her keep me around...It's pathetic, I know. But I'll take what I can get.

Fortunately I was given little time for self-pity. Summer kept us busy.

We stopped whenever one of us spotted an interesting mushroom. It was usually Summer that found them. I had never realized there were so many of them in the forest til she pointed them out. How many times had I walked through these woods and never even noticed them? It was kind of sad.

So many different colors, shapes, and forms and I would have missed out on them completely if I'd never been invited to go foraging with Summer. I guess that's the power of interacting with other people; they can open doors for you that you would never have thought to even try the handle of to see if they were unlocked.

To think, when we first left out on this vacation, I thought Summer might be too pampered and sheltered to enjoy being out in nature. I had thought she'd be unable to handle the woods full of insects, all the dirt and mud, not to mention the lack of air conditioning.

Summer had proven me wrong in every way. She moved through the woods like some kind of fairy creature, a dryad maybe, and managed to teach Aidan and I a thing or two, showing us new elements of woods we'd been in many times before.

I should never have underestimated her. I would have to try harder in the future to not fall prey to assumptions.

Aidan didn't seem to have joined me in my newfound admiration of Summer's outdoors' skills. He was showing a distinct lack of appreciation for her work as a foraging guide for us.

"How much longer do we have to do this?" he whined.

"Until my basket is full." Summer said, patting the little basket she'd brought along.

"Friggin' omega dictator...Jess, if you weren't so whipped we could stage a revolt." Aidan grumbled.

I shot him a glare, but my attention was pulled away from chewing him out over that comment when Summer stuck an arm out in front of us to halt our progress.

"Stop here. Those are black trumpet mushrooms." Summer said, pointing to a little cluster of brownish–gray mushrooms that were growing in the leaf litter of the forest floor.

I dutifully began collecting them.

"What do you want these for anyway? Mushrooms are nasty." Aidan said.

"You're such a child," Summer said, "mushrooms are delicious and a good meat alternative if you're a vegetarian."

Aidan made a face. "Just another of the million reasons why I will never become a vegetarian."

We walked a little further and collected a few more kinds of mushrooms, but the sun was climbing high in the sky overhead. We had to have been at it for hours. I checked my watch. It was afternoon.

"We can stop," Summer said, noticing what I

was doing. "I'm getting pretty tired from all this walking."

"Did the heat take a lot out of you?" Aidan asked, as we turned around to head back to the campgrounds.

I wasn't sure if he was talking about the heat she'd went through as an omega or being out under the hot broiling sun. Probably the first one.

"Yeah. But I'll bounce back pretty soon. I'll have more energy tomorrow after a day of actually getting to eat something." Summer answered.

The walk back to the campgrounds passed much quicker than our walk out into the woods, since we didn't have to stop in random spots to pull up mushrooms. (We did have to stop to take photos of a cute turtle that crossed our path. It was a natural hazard of traveling through the forest.)

When we got back to the cabins, Mom and Dad were nowhere to be seen. With the long trail they'd picked for today's hike, they probably wouldn't be back until late in the evening. That meant lunch was on us, and all of us were hungry after the hours spent foraging.

"I'm going to fry up some of these mushrooms. Do you want some Jessica?" Summer asked me.

"Blegh. Count me out." Aidan said, making a face.

"I didn't ask you. I asked Jessica." Summer said.

"Sure, I'd like that." I said.

Booyeah! What a cool and normal response I'd given. But not too cool. What a tricky balance.

"I guess it's sandwiches for me." Aidan said sadly.

We both ignored him.

Summer walked up to her cabin and unlocked the door. She propped it open and went inside. I followed after her.

"Is there anything I can do to help?" I asked.

The last thing I wanted to do was give Summer the impression I was one of those alphas who thinks omegas are supposed to wait on them hand and foot, while we just lounged around and did nothing.

"If you want, you can pat these dry after I rinse them." Summer said, gesturing to the mushroom basket she'd sat on the counter.

She started pulling mushrooms out.

"You don't trust me with anything more complicated?" I asked.

"It's nothing personal. These are delicacies, they require a special touch." she said, with a touch of haughtiness.

I snorted. Then I went to stand by her at the sink, and we got to work. Her hands were wet and cool against mine as she passed me the rinsed mushrooms so I could pat them dry with paper towels.

After a few minutes, the sound of hiking boots tromping inside the cabin pulled my gaze away from Summer. Aidan walked through the kitchen doorway, his arms full of the fixings for sandwiches. He plunked his loaf of bread and sandwich bags of meat and vegetables down on the kitchen table.

"You two want any of this?" he asked.

I weaved around her to the other side of the kitchen to get what she'd requested from the shelves on the far wall. I brought them over to her and she began pouring olive oil into the skillet.

"Quite the picture of domesticity you two are." Aidan remarked.

"Shut up and give me that sandwich." I said, taking a seat at the table across from him.

"Summer?" Aidan called.

Summer was humming quietly as she stirred the mushrooms. I held out my hand to Aidan.

"I see how it is. You stole my best friend so now there's no one to protect me from your bullying." he sniffed, but he finally handed me my sandwich.

I started eating it, but I barely tasted the food I was chewing. I was watching Summer as she moved around the kitchen, cooking up a whole batch of mushrooms. The smell of herbs and garlic sautéing was mouthwatering.

Aidan smirked knowingly at me.

"What?" I asked.

"You are so clueless." he said.

The urge to pull the pickle slices off my sandwich and fling them at him was strong, but I resisted. It was a tough battle. Only the risk of earning Summer's disapproval convinced me to behave like an adult. She might get pissed if I started a food fight with my dumbass brother in her kitchen, especially while she was cooking in it.

Eventually my patience and good behavior was rewarded. Summer walked over carrying two plates full of steaming hot mushrooms for us to eat.

I smiled when I saw she had taken an equally big serving for herself. She really did need to eat to make up for the meals she had missed during her heat. Aidan made himself another sandwich, while I declined a second one since I had mushrooms to eat.

We tucked into our food, finishing it fast. We had all exercised a lot earlier and had worked up quite an appetite.

Once we had polished off all the mushrooms and sandwich fixings (and we did convince Summer to have one, although it was just lettuce and mushrooms on bread) we were stuffed to the gills. We lounged around the cabin in a food-induced stupor for a while.

We chatted lazily about seemingly nothing at all, until Aidan's drowsy eyes landed on the *Castles of Insanity* box that was still sitting out on the coffee table.

"Oh man, you brought that dumb game with you? I can't believe you tormented Summer with it while she was weak and defenseless from her heat." Aidan said to me.

"Tormented? She likes it too!" I said.

"It's true." Summer said. "The jury is out, and you're the lame one for not liking it Aidan."

"Oh my God, she's brainwashed you!" Aidan said, covering his face with his hands. "I'm so sorry Summer, I should've watched out for you. Should've protected you from my evil big sis..."

"Why haven't we drowned him in the river yet?" Summer asked me.

"Ate too much, it's too far to walk now." I answered.

She laughed, and I couldn't help but glow a little. The sound was like music to my ears.

"Come on Aidan, we'll start a new game and you can play." Summer said.

"No way!" he said. "We have the beautiful, great outdoors waiting for us, and you want to sit inside your cabin and play a board game?"

"You owe it to me for referring to me as 'weak' and 'defenseless'." She countered, putting her hands on her hips.

"Yeah, I was wrong. You're definitely not defenseless." Aidan muttered.

When she leaned toward him threateningly, he threw his hands up in surrender.

"Fine, fine. I'll play the dumb game with you guys. But seriously, can't it wait for another time?" he asked.

The teasing grin slipped off of Summer's face like it had never been there.

"I don't have it in me to do any more physical activities like swimming or hiking right now. It's not that I don't want to." Summer said.

Summer looked so downtrodden, it made an answering pang resound in my chest. I felt so bad for her. Sure, she'd gotten a lucky break in her heat ending early enough for her to enjoy some of her vacation, but it had still robbed her of valuable time off. She'd been deprived of days she should have been frolicking in the woods full of energy and laughs.

At least my brother wasn't completely oblivious to how badly he'd misstepped. He caved without another word.

"Okay," Aidan said, "how about we play one round, and then reassess your energy levels?"

"Deal." Summer said, putting her hand out for him to shake, and they shook on it.

With that decided, we started unpacking and setting up the game. Soon, even Aidan was sucked into the game play. He ended up getting so engrossed he forgot to check in with Summer and see if her energy levels had recovered. By the end of the game session, he even admitted it "wasn't that bad" and that he'd play it again.

But there was no question of playing another of the game's scenarios tonight, or heading outside to do something. Summer was barely keeping her eyes open. Her lids kept drifting down to rest for a moment, then she'd catch herself and they'd flutter open, looking as if they were pushing up against the weight of anvils.

"Better get to bed before Jessica has to carry you there." Aidan advised.

I blushed. The imagery was nice though. I would have loved to princess carry Summer into her bedroom.

"Alright, alright. I'll see you two tomorrow then." Summer said, failing to stifle a yawn.

She pushed herself up to her feet, swaying a little, and headed towards the bathroom. I glanced at the window. It was getting dark outside.

Aidan started towards the door, motioning for me to follow. I stared at him. What did he want me to come outside for...?

"Oh! Duh!" I said, smacking myself on the forehead with the edge of my palm.

I wasn't supposed to be spending the night in Summer's cabin again, curled up with her. That was over. It was time for me to spend my first night alone in my own bed. I wanted to grumble; my own lonely bed didn't seem anywhere near as inviting. But I couldn't think of a good reason to stick around Summer's place for another night, so I followed my brother out of the cabin.

I stood on the threshold for a moment, and called "Good night Summer!" into her cabin.

I heard a muffled "Night!" float out from the bathroom.

I closed the door carefully behind me, thinking about the omega inside getting ready for bed.

CHAPTER 10: JESSICA

The rest of our vacation passed by in a blur. I mean that in a good way, it was like someone snapped their fingers and everything flew by in fast-forward. They say time flies when you're having fun, and we had lots of it.

We spent our days swimming in the river, just splashing around. We went foraging again for berries and mushrooms and edible roots. We went on hikes to summits high up in the mountains, looking out on incredible views.

We didn't have a care in the world, and we laughed and joked with each other like we'd known each other our whole lives. Well okay, that was actually true with me and Aidan, since we were siblings close in age. And since Aidan and Summer had been friends since Kindergarten we'd both known her for most of our lives.

So technically I'd known her that long, but I'd never *gotten* to know her. Our relationship before this trip was more like a lengthy but distant acquaintanceship.

We didn't tire of each other's company now, but by the very last day of the trip, it had begun to feel like we'd done all there was to do.

We'd just finished breakfast, and were sitting around the picnic table fanning ourselves with paper plates and trying to decide what we would do that day.

"Why don't we just go fishing with Mom and Dad? We haven't done that yet." Aidan said.

Summer scoffed. "Uhh, I'm a vegetarian, duh?"

"You can catch and release them!" Aidan said.

She rolled her eyes. "I'm still not going to shove a metal hook through some poor fish's mouth. It's barbaric."

"You're barbaric." Aidan said.

We fanned ourselves a little more and wracked our brains for something to cap off our trip.

"How about we go check out the cave?" I asked.

There was a tourist trap cave a couple miles from the campsite. Aidan and I had both been there before on past trips.

"Fairy Cave? It's so lame. It's not even a good cave." Aidan said, wrinkling his nose.

"It's more exciting than *fishing*." I said.

It's true. Not that I mind fishing, but the only part

of it I enjoyed was sitting in a boat with my family talking and watching nature. I wasn't crazy about seafood or angling so it wasn't exactly thrilling for me.

Summer leaned forward, her eyes meeting mine across the table.

"I'd like to see a cave. I'd never been in one before." she said.

Ha! Take that Aidan. Summer was picking my idea, clearly it was the superior option.

"Just skip this one, it'll only disappoint you." Aidan said.

"You're such a hater. It's not that bad, it's not like every cave can be the most amazing thing in the world. They're natural formations, not something designed for entertaining humans." I said, sticking up for the little cave.

It really wasn't bad or anything. I wouldn't have suggested it if it was truly boring or lacking in any redeeming qualities. It just wasn't as big or as magnificent as some of the larger caves in the state.

"Well you two can go to the lame cave if you want. I'm going to go fishing." Aidan said.

Summer snorted. "Fine. You'll probably regret that when you don't catch anything."

"Hey! I'll have you know I'm a master angler."

Aidan said. "I'm going to catch so many fish and show you."

"Sure Aidan, sure." Summer said, shaking her head.

I laughed.

***

Mom and Dad offered us a ride, but Summer and I chose to walk the couple of miles to the cave. Sitting in a car was something we could do anytime, but walking through the woods was something I only got to do a couple weeks a year, and Summer pretty much never got to until now.

It didn't take us long to reach the cave site. There wasn't an exposed, bare cave opening to see. The owners of the land had had a building constructed over it, a huge gift shop where you could sign up for tours or buy loads of overpriced souvenirs.

The gift shop was packed full, there was probably a hundred people in there. The air was noisy with the sound of families and couples chatting to each other as they perused the offerings.

Summer wanted to look at everything, and there was a lot to look at. Since there were tours every thirty minutes I didn't see any reason to rush her.

I'd seen it all before, but I liked talking about the items with Summer, seeing what she liked or thought was lame. There were hundreds of colorful animal plushies and cool rocks and gemstones.

After looking at everything, neither of us had found anything we absolutely had to buy, so we went ahead and signed up for the next tour.

It would have made more sense to do that before we looked around, but fortunately our tour group was just about to leave out anyway, so we didn't have to wait long.

When our group was called over the intercom, we all gathered around the door leading to the cave. The guide gave us a brief history of the discovery of the cave (which I tuned out because I had heard it several times before), and the usual cave safety precautions.

Finally, he unlocked the door behind him. I stuck close to Summer as our group followed him down a long twisting staircase.

I had to duck my head down to avoid whacking it on the craggy rocks that formed the ceiling overhead. I looked enviously at Summer, who didn't have to stoop over at all and could walk blithely along. The benefits of being half a foot shorter than me.

She glanced around at everything, drinking in the sight of the bumpy cave walls.

"Make sure you hold onto the railing, the stairs are really slick." I said.

Crap, was I being and overbearing an overprotective alpha again? Would she think I was condescending to her by giving her a warning of something she probably already noticed herself and might consider obvious?

The water on the stairs was visible to anyone who looked down, although the lights strung along the path weren't strong enough to make it apparent otherwise.

But Summer nodded and said "Right." and moved her hand to graze along the railing as she walked down. My shoulders slumped, releasing a tension I hadn't even realized I was holding.

After a couple of minutes of steady descent, we came out into a small, level cavern. I knew we hadn't gotten into the cave proper yet, we were simply on the cusp of it.

Across the cavern there was a hole ringed with stalagmites and stalactites. That was the entrance we would walk through to begin the proper cave tour. The guide led us to it.

"You'll have to take a big step to get through here, really stretch your leg over, but if you need to, you can rest your hand along the wall here." The tour guide said, pointing to a patch of cave wall that was an ugly gray from having been touched by so many human hands (the rest of the cave wall was a healthy warm orange hue). The oils in human skin damages cave structures.

Getting through this entrance was the only tricky part of navigating this cave. But I'd managed it even as a small child, so it was doable.

I didn't expect Summer to have any problems, so I wasn't paying that much attention when she moved through the entrance. But Summer failed the big step. She started out alright, stretching one leg forward to touch the ground on the other side of the rocks and spikes sticking up. But when she moved her back leg forward to finish the step, her feet slipped out from under her.

I don't know if it was because she wasn't used to the odd surface of the cave floor, or hadn't taken the guide's warning seriously.

Without even thinking, I rushed forward and threw my arms around her torso, hauling her back before she could fall onto the spiky rocks. She was so small and light, her back pressed against my chest.

"Fuck, are you okay?!" I asked.

She wasn't moving, still as a statue, just blinking dazedly at me.

"Yeah...I guess the ground was just slippier than I expected." she said.

Or were her muscles weak from the heat she'd experienced at the start of our vacation? She should be recovered by now. She'd been swimming and hiking all week without any problems, other than tiring easily on the first day her heat ended.

Still, I'd better keep an eye on her just in case.

She finally pulled out of my grasp, brushing herself off.

"Okay, let's try that again. This time, I'll be more careful." Summer said.

She glanced at me, smiling. "And I know you're ready to catch me if it goes wrong."

The brightness of her smile was blinding. My heart pounded in my chest. I felt a little dizzy now myself, being on the receiving end of that affectionate gaze. Oh, to be looked at like that! There was really nothing better.

I watched as Summer turned back towards the cave entrance, taking her smile with her. She braced one hand against the wall this time, and I held my breath. My nervousness was for nothing though. This time she made the large step successfully. Now it was my turn.

With my longer legs stretching over the spiky rocks wasn't hard, although I had to kind of limbo my torso backwards to not hit my head on the ones coming down from the ceiling. And then our group continued on.

It wasn't a very long tour, and I spent most of it tuning out the tour guide. I looked at the cave formations and thought about the long history of the cave and the thousands of people who had visited it throughout the years.

Back in the nineteenth century, had there been an alpha girl like me and an omega girl like Summer that had explored this cave? We were both kind of weird but the twenty-first century doesn't have a monopoly on weird women.

Summer though, was paying rapt attention to the tour guide's words. I tuned back in for a second.

"The population growth in this area has lead to increased pollution in the runoff, which damages the cave's fragile ecosystem—"

Ahh. No wonder she was interested.

It wasn't all alarming environmentalist updates though. The guide also explained what kind of wildlife lived in the cave and how the formations had been created. That was more interesting, but the cave was still kind of warm and humid and I was getting bored.

I didn't regret visiting the cave though, since Summer was enjoying it. There was no way she would've liked fishing, and if I'd went with Aidan and she didn't then she'd have been left with no company all day.

That is, if Mom even would have let her go off by herself. Summer is a young omegan woman after all. I suppose I should be pleased that Mom thinks I am an appropriate chaperone for her. Especially after she saw me coming out of Summer's cabin.

A blush crept up my face, even though I knew I had done nothing to feel embarrassed about. We'd done none of the things dirty minds would automatically imagine when they heard an omega and an alpha were alone together.

But I couldn't keep my fingers from straying up to touch my lips, remembering the feeling of Summer pressed against them.

I distracted myself by paying attention to the tour guide once more, but the tour seemed to be wrapping up. We were led back along the path and up the stairs, heading towards the entrance to the gift shop. Our return was uneventful, and we left behind the mysterious and beautiful underground world for the more mundane modern setting of bustling shoppers and gift shop shelves.

"So what do you think?" I asked Summer, as we made a beeline for the doors.

We stepped out into fresh air and bright sunlight. It had gotten even hotter, now well into the afternoon.

"That was amazing! I loved it. If that's what Aidan calls a small lame cave, I can't wait to see the big amazing ones." Summer said.

I smiled. "One of the largest ones in the state is pretty close to the university, if you're interested in going sometime."

There, that was natural wasn't it? I was just

offering to see a cave with her. Not asking to form a mate-bond or elope or anything.

"Yeah? That would be awesome. We should totally go when we head back upstate for the semester." Summer said.

A thrill ran through me. Yes! She hadn't thought it was a weird offer to make and was totally down to go caving with me again. With this and the shopping trip she'd asked me on, we were sure to be spending some together after this vacation was over. I was so elated I wanted to shout. I had to fight to keep a huge goofy grin off my face.

We started back towards the cabins, sticking to the woods while keeping the road in our sights. We strolled in companionable silence, admiring the scenery around us but making good time.

Until Summer stopped all of sudden, throwing an arm out to signal to me to halt.

"What is it?" I asked.

My eyes darted around, searching for anything that might be alarming or dangerous. Summer walked over to a patch of forest a few yards away. I followed her. She was examining something in front of her. I peered around her.

What had caught Summer's eye was a large clump of black-eyed Susans, almost waist-high, their bright yellow petals waving gently in the light breeze.

Summer began to pick a few of them, her pale slender fingers wrapping around their stems and breaking them off. When she gathered a few, she turned to me.

I just raised an eyebrow, and waited to see what she was up to. She leaned forward, and tucked one of the flowers over my ear. Then she leaned back, examining me, her gaze serious and heavy. Then her face abruptly lightened as she laughed, pleased with the effect.

"Thanks." I said wryly.

Seeing her, laughing in the warm summer sun, so healthy and alive and happy, all her attention on me, I felt like my heart would burst from my chest. I was seized by a wild urge to take hold of her shoulders and kiss her. Fiercely, but I knew that if I really did it I wouldn't be fierce, but rather soft.

The desire was edged with a sharp pain, the hurt of wanting something so much and knowing you can't have it.

This wasn't working, my feelings of attraction to Summer weren't going away. I'd been telling myself all week that her and I could just be friends, that she would want nothing to do with me other than that. And maybe, probably, that was true. Why would she, or any omega, want to be with me romantically?

But was it right, to keep being around her while

keeping up a false front? While pretending that I had no interest like that? It seemed kind of skeevy, and I didn't even know if I'd be able to keep it up.

Maybe being around her as a friend and watching her date other people would be too painful. Then I'd have to break the friendship, and that would be cruel to her, who had done nothing wrong.

Maybe it would be better to just confess, to get the rejection out of the way now. Make her never want to be around me, have her relegate me to a background role once more, just Aidan's annoying older sister again.

"Summer, I have something to tell you." I said.

She began tying one of the black-eyed Susans into her own hair. The dark brown center of the flower stood out sharply amongst her short pale locks.

"What is it?" Summer asked.

She wasn't giving me her full attention, probably assuming I was going to tell her something mundane.

"I know this is probably not what you want to hear. And that you may even be disgusted with me for what I'm going to tell you, but I have to be honest." I started.

Her gaze shifted from the flower she'd been adjusting, to my face, the full weight of her attention settling on me like an overloaded mountaineer's backpack, threatening to send me tumbling down. I could only sweat and internally writhe under the pressure.

Her arms rested loosely at her sides as she waited for me to speak, the flowers now forgotten.

I had to say something. Just spit it out Jessica! Like lancing a boil, it would be painful but it had to be done.

"I like you...a lot." I managed to sputter.

"I like you a lot too?" Summer said, tilting her head. "You're definitely not the dork I thought you were. You're an even bigger dork, but in a super cool way."

"No, I mean I like *like* you." I said, barely able to force the words out. I could feel myself beginning to tremble, the adrenaline and nerves catching up to me.

"Oh." she said. "Oh!" her eyes widened.

"I swear I didn't feel this way before we spent your heat together. I wouldn't have agreed to be your heat-partner if I'd known I was attracted to you. Not that it was the heat that made me start liking you! I'm not that kind of alpha! It was the time spent with you, getting to know you." I spluttered out.

Summer grinned. My heart sank.

Of course the idea of me nurturing an attraction to someone like her was laughable. She was way out of my league and knew it. Now she would tell me she couldn't believe it, or maybe what a big idiot I was. I'm sure her and Aidan would have a huge laugh over this once we got back to the campsite.

But when she opened her mouth, what came out wasn't either of those.

 "God, I am so glad you said something." she said.

Huh?

"I think I feel the same way. Only I never would have had the guts to say anything. Seriously, I was going to take this crush to my grave." Summer said.

"What? There is no way you like-like me." I said.

She must be joking, doing the first prank of many that her and Aidan would put me through over this.

"I just told you I did." Summer said, shrugging. "Don't tell me how I feel." her eyes locked onto mine, turning fiery during that last part.

"Summer, don't say these things if you don't mean them." I warned.

"Hey, I'm serious. I wouldn't fuck around with your feelings like that. I'm not that big a jerk. I'm not making any promises, I really haven't dated much or had a lot of romantic experience, so I could be totally mistaken. But I think that I really like you, and I'd love to see us try and make it work." she said.

I couldn't believe what I was hearing. Could someone, let alone an amazing gorgeous omega like Summer, really like me? There was only one way to find out.

"Can I kiss you?" I asked.

"I've been wanting you to kiss me like a hundred times this week." she said, leaning forward.

It wasn't the overwhelmingly passionate or lustfilled panting kiss I'd pictured. I didn't sweep her in my arms and kiss every inch of her body or anything. We just leaned forward, and our lips touched lightly. She was wearing some kind of lip gloss, and it smelled like strawberries. It was better though, than those grand kisses I'd been imagining. It was sweet and laid-back, with sparks of desire as our tongues lightly explored each other's mouth.

Our first real kiss, without an omega's heat to excuse it. This could be the first of many. God I hoped so. My first girlfriend! I was so excited.

When we broke the kiss, I couldn't stop grinning. She took my hand in hers, and our arms swung gently together as we continued walking back to the campsite.

"You know, if you keep smiling like that, everyone is going to know what happened when we get back there." Summer said.

She was smiling too, although it was more subdued than my idiotic grin.

"Is that a problem?" I asked, genuinely curious.

Would she want us to keep it a secret for a while, make sure the relationship was going to work out before she told anyone? Was she worried about what her parents would think, and whether they would try to keep us apart?

I wasn't the worst potential alpha suitor—I was in college, and would have a good respectable career one day, and would treat their daughter right—but I wasn't the best either. There were smarter, richer, more debonair alphas out there. Ones who weren't awkward and weird...

Summer broke me out of my musings before they could get too negative.

"It's not a problem for me at all. I can't wait to tell everyone. Aidan is going to die when he finds out." she said, her smile widening into a full-on grin at the thought.

I laughed. It was true, my brother would flip his shit—if he believed us and didn't take it for a prank of our own.

As for the rest of my family...I'm sure Mom wouldn't mind me dating Summer, not when she saw I was serious about it. And I already knew Dad was rooting for romance. I didn't know Summer's parents well, but I would do my best to win them over.

It's funny; when the semester ended, I hadn't been looking forward to our summer break at all. Back then I couldn't wait to get it over with, so I could get back to college and knock out the classes I needed to get my degree.

But now I'm looking forward to every day of it. I couldn't wait to spend the summer going on silly little dates with my girlfriend. We'd get milkshakes, see movies together, and just lay around and complain about how hot it was outside.

We would play through each other's collection of board games and I would listen to her rant about the environment and she would listen to me ramble about my senior research project.

I'd find out all her favorite foods and what kinds of music she liked, and she would learn mine.

And when the semester finally started we'd spend our evenings studying together. We'd meet up between classes to get coffee together at the campus cafe. We'd spend hours in bed when the leaves turned and it got cold, snuggled up warm together under the covers. There would be thousands of kisses shared and maybe more.

I smiled. Yeah, it was going to be great.

EPILOGUE: SUMMER

The air was stifling hot and the katydids were loud in the trees as we floated down the river. It could have been the summer we fell in love if not for a few minor differences. I'd dyed my hair a very pale purple a few days before our trip, and Jessica had taken to keeping her long brown hair in braids this year.

She had the same blue swimsuit on as a year before, but I had on a black one piece with a little attached skirt. It had been a bad purchase, the black made me look washed out, but Jess was the kind of adoring love-sotted alpha who could never tell me the truth about whether I looked good in the clothing I tried on. It was great at times but it had its downsides.

"You look good in everything!" she'd say earnestly when I complained about it.

It had been bought during our first mall shopping trip together, so I suppose it had sentimental value even if it was the opposite of flattering. It wasn't the only mark of our relationship I was wearing. The faint bite mark on my scent gland might have seemed as superficial and trivial as hair style changes or a new bathing suit, but to me it meant everything.

It was not just a colossal change, it was a universe-cracking one for me. Even as the canoe bobbed along, and Jessica's voice floated over to me as she rambled about frog facts, I couldn't help but take a moment to rest my paddle on the canoe, the better to free up my hand so I could run my fingers over the mark.

It was a mate mark. I'd given Jessica an identical one, although it was unconventional and against every tradition for an omega to bite their alpha back.

The two bite marks were something I'd always thought I'd never see—that there would never be the day where I'd find an alpha I could trust to mark me as theirs, and that I'd never find an open-minded alpha who was willing to let me do the same to them, marking us as equals and belonging to each other, not just me to them.

I wanted to say as much to Jessica, but she was in the middle of repeating over and over again how adorable pumpkin toadlets are.

"They're just so cute! I have to have one Summer!" Jessica gushed.

"No way am I letting you be one of those assholes who illegally imports exotic pets," I said, "leave the pumpkin toadlet where it belongs—in Brazil."

At this point I was more than used to my girlfriend getting on random kicks where she'd obsess over something. I only had myself to blame for this one —I'd been the one who made us watch videos online of cool weird animals one day, about a month ago.

Thus introducing her to the tiny orange frog, and unknowingly, her latest hyperfixation.

I didn't have to turn around from my position at the front of the canoe, to know that she was pouting at my words.

"You know, I bet it's not too late to change my research focus from neurobiology to batrachology." Jessica said.

Batrochology being the study of amphibians, which I knew from my own environmental science classes and from being refreshed by Jessica's latest obsession.

"Bullshit. You'll be over frogs by September, while your fascination for the human brain will never end." I said.

"You say that but the pumpkin toadlet will live in my heart forever!" Jessica insisted.

"I can't believe I have competition—and from a silly frog smaller than my thumb." I said.

"I promise I'll never give the toadlet a bite—it's too small for that." Jessica said.

I smiled, hearing that the mating bites were still on her mind as well. We'd given them to each other two weeks ago, on our one-year anniversary.

Most people did consider it a major life milestone, but it was kind of ironic that it was such a big deal to me and still made me glow inside to think about. I'd always rolled my eyes at omegas who acted like getting a mate mark was the highest goal an omega could achieve, and their wedding the pinnacle of their life.

Not that Jess and I were married, or anywhere close to it—we'd both agreed we wanted to be done with school first—and with Jessica heading for grad school that wasn't any time soon. The mate marks were a precursor to marriage, a formal mark of engagement.

I was in the weird position of being an omega who had to make their peace with their own excitement and joy over these things. Society expected us to feel that way about our relationships, and pushed it, and I'd had lots to say (a book's worth, easily) about omegas' worth being boiled down to their marriage and family, about the wedding industry and the sexist and capitalist ideas it profited off of, and my problems with pretty much every wedding tradition.

But after a lot of soul-searching (and persistent prodding from Jessica over having my "broody face" on so much after the bite mark ceremony) I'd come to realize my joy wasn't due to some internalization of toxic social expectations that reduced my own worth. My happiness was instead my triumph over a poisoning I hadn't even known I'd suffered. Society's invasive and narrow-minded beliefs about omegas had sent me running from love because it had made it into a cage for people like me.

I had thought I had to be alone to be free.

In being able to love Jessica freely and healthily, I'd taken back something that should have always been mine.

I would never speak these words aloud because Aidan would give me so much shit over them. "Only you could make an omega marrying an alpha out to be some kind of subversive-transgressive political act Summer!" he'd say.

I couldn't believe he was going to be my brother-in-law. Well, I'd show him. My wedding would be super badass and not traditional at all (other than the traditions Jessica and I liked). I'd even decided to invite my parents, because it would be funny as shit to watch my mother cringe at the absolute inversion of the perfect princess wedding she'd no doubt been dreaming of for me since I was a baby.

I must've been quiet for a while because Jessica broke the silence.

"What are you thinking about Summer?" she asked.

"Whether a black or red wedding dress would piss my mother off more." I replied.

"The answer, I think, is a tux." Jessica said.

"Oh, you're probably right. How do you feel about wearing a dress? It would probably make her blow a gasket." I said.

Jessica laughed. "I'm not opposed. I figured I'd leave my wardrobe up to you, as always. Although if you're wanting to horrify your mother, maybe you should let me pick it out for that day. Then again, I don't want to look truly bad on my own wedding day..."

"Sweetheart, you'd look good in a burlap bag. But we'll get you something nice." I said.

I leaned over the side of the canoe a little to splash some water on my face—yeah, it was river water, but it's not like I was drinking the stuff. It was nice and cool on my sun warmed skin.

Unfortunately, that's when Jessica must have felt like

being romantic and stretched forward in the canoe, because I felt her arms around my waist and then she was kissing my cheek.

We still would have been okay, but at that moment the canoe scraped over a massive rock, and began tilting in the direction I was leaned towards. Panicking, I pushed Jessica back and lunged for my paddle.

I wasn't quick enough. It was like everything was moving in slow-motion, but I wasn't fast enough to change anything. The whole canoe tipped over. A second later everything speeded back up, as I plunged down into the water.

I resurfaced rapidly—it wasn't hard, the water was only waist deep here and I got my feet against the river bottom soon enough.

"Jess! Are you okay?!" I shouted, my head whipping around as I looked for my girlfriend.

The water might have been shallow, but that rock had been huge. If Jessica had hit her head on it—

Something broke the water's surface near the upside-down canoe. Wet droplets streaming down water-blackened brown hair—Jessica.

I moved towards her.

"I'm okay!" she said, gasping. "I landed under the canoe."

I grabbed her, wrapping my arms around her and squeezing her hard.

"Damn, that scared the shit out of me." Jessica said, returning my hug.

"You were scared? *You* were scared?" I drew back from the hug and glared at her.

"Hey, I wasn't the one who leaned over the side of the canoe—"

"You leaned all the way up against me! You're the one who overbalanced it—"

As we playfully argued, we didn't even notice as the canoe floated further downstream.

Such a typical summer day for us. And I wouldn't change a bit of it.

AFTERWORD

I hope that you enjoyed reading *Up an Omegaverse Creek Without a Paddle* as much as I enjoyed writing it.

If you liked this story, please consider leaving a rating or review for it. It can really help an author out!

Made in United States
Troutdale, OR
05/16/2024

19922405R00119